The Beginning

MARILYN KAYE

BANTAM BOOKS
NEW YORK • TORONTO • LONDON • SYDNEY • AUCKLAND

RL 5.5, 008–012

THE BEGINNING

A Bantam Skylark Book / October 2000

ISBN 0-553-48715-9

Visit us on the Web! www.randomhouse.com/kids

Published simultaneously in the United States and Canada

Bantam Skylark is an imprint of Random House Children's Books, a division of Random House, Inc. SKYLARK BOOK and colophon and BANTAM BOOKS and colophon are registered trademarks of Random House, Inc. Bantam Books, 1540 Broadway, New York, New York 10036.

PRINTED IN THE UNITED STATES OF AMERICA

OPM   10   9   8   7   6   5   4   3   2   1

For my dear friend,
Jacki Marino

The Beginning

one

At the front of the classroom, the boy rapped a gavel on the desk. "I hereby call this meeting of the Parkside Middle School Student Council to order."

Immediately Amy could feel her eyelids begin to droop. She always had a hard time staying awake during these meetings. If she had only known how boring the student council would be, she would never have run in the election. But she had run, and she had won, and it was too late for regrets. She was now one of eighteen representatives, all of whom looked like they were about to fall asleep too.

Except maybe for Carrie Nolan, another rep from

the seventh grade. There was a twitchy little smile on her face, as if she had some sort of secret. But Amy figured that if Carrie knew something special, it couldn't possibly have anything to do with student council. The most exciting news that month had been about someone dropping plastic bottles in the paper recycling bins.

After calling the meeting to order, President Cliff Fields directed the secretary to read the minutes of the previous meeting. That took all of about thirty seconds. The minutes were approved, the vice-president called the roll, the treasurer gave the budget report, and the president called for old business. Since nothing had happened at the last meeting, there wasn't any old business.

"Is there any new business?" Cliff asked. There wasn't much hope in his voice.

But a hand actually went up. Surprised, Cliff said, "The president recognizes Carrie Nolan."

Carrie rose. "As chair of the student travel committee, I have been asked by Dr. Noble to meet with all seventh-grade student council representatives. We're supposed to decide where the seventh grade will go for the annual class trip."

"What's the big deal?" Cliff asked. "The seventh grade always goes to the state capital."

Amy could tell by the twinkle in Carrie's eyes that

she was about to spill her secret. "Not this year," Carrie said. "We don't even have to stay in California. Dr. Noble said that Parkside got a special grant for student travel, and there's enough money for the seventh grade to go anywhere in the United States."

Cliff stared at her in disbelief. "No way."

"Yes way," Carrie replied. "All the seventh-grade reps should stay after this meeting so we can choose a place for our trip."

A ninth-grade representative exploded. "That's not fair! When I was in the seventh grade, we had to go to Sacramento."

"Yeah, so did we," echoed an eighth-grader. "What about the other grades? Are we getting special trips?"

"No, nothing else changes," Carrie replied. "Only the seventh grade goes on an annual class trip, just like always."

"That stinks!" someone yelled. "Why should this year's seventh grade get better treatment?"

Carrie grinned. "You want to go tell Dr. Noble this isn't fair?" There were more than a few snickers in the room. Nobody, not even the student council president, would have the gall to complain to their intimidating principal that this year's seventh grade was getting a special deal.

There was no more new business, so the meeting

was adjourned. As the eighth- and ninth-grade representatives left, many of them shot envious looks at the six seventh-graders who stayed behind.

"Go to Hawaii," one of them advised before leaving.

"Can we?" Justin Kelly asked Carrie. "Hawaii sounds great."

"What about Alaska?" Molly Cohn wanted to know.

"I'm not sure," Carrie said. "Dr. Noble said anywhere in the U.S., but I think that means just the states that are attached."

"It would," Justin grumbled.

"Oh, shut up," Carrie replied. "Who's got a serious idea?"

"Orlando, Florida," Max Barstow declared. "Disney World."

"Yeah, super idea!" Larry Moore exclaimed. "We could go to Universal Studios and the beaches."

"That's crazy," Molly objected. "We've got Disney-*land* right in Anaheim. And movie studios, and plenty of beaches too."

"Yeah, but everyone's sick of the Pacific Ocean," Max argued. "In Florida, you've got the Atlantic."

"And the Gulf of Mexico," Larry added.

Carrie shook her head. "It's gotta be someplace educational, guys."

4

Amy visualized a map of the United States and considered the possibilities. "How about the Southwest?" she suggested. "The Grand Canyon, the Petrified Forest. Indian reservations."

"Lots of kids have gone on vacations there," Molly pointed out.

"Then what about the Rocky Mountains?" Amy asked. "A hiking trip would be cool."

"*Everyone's* gone hiking in the Rocky Mountains," Justin said. "Okay, maybe not everyone, but I think most kids would rather go to a city."

"How about New York?" Larry asked.

Max yawned. "Been there, done that."

Carrie frowned. "We're not choosing a place just for *you*, Max."

Amy had a thought. "You guys ever been to Washington, D.C.?"

That got a buzz going. Everyone started talking at once, about the White House, and the Smithsonian, and all the sights of the nation's capital. "I've got a pen pal on the East Coast," Molly said, "and she says D.C. is the most popular place for East Coast kids to go on class trips."

"Have any of you been there before?" Carrie asked.

They all shook their heads—except Amy.

"You've been to Washington?" Carrie asked her.

"Yes, sort of. I was . . . I was born in D.C. But I left when I was a baby, so I don't remember anything."

Born . . . that was the best word she could come up with to describe what had happened in Washington, D.C., almost thirteen years ago. She couldn't very well tell her classmates that she had been *created* there.

Washington, D.C. A tingling began in her heart and spread throughout her body. The sensation wasn't simply a reaction to the idea of seeing the White House, or the Pentagon, or any of the capital's other major sights. It came from the notion of seeing where it had all begun. Where *she* had begun.

So when the seventh-grade reps took a vote, Amy joined the majority in enthusiastic support for Washington as the destination for the class trip. Of course, their decision was subject to the principal's approval, but Amy didn't think there would be any problem. Dr. Noble might have objected to Disney World, but there was no denying the educational value of the nation's capital.

That was why Amy felt pretty confident at lunchtime, when she told her best friend, Tasha Morgan, about the plans for the class trip.

"Washington!" Tasha squealed.

"Shhh," Amy hissed. "It's not official yet. But if

Dr. Noble approves our suggestion, she'll announce it tomorrow."

Tasha obediently lowered her voice. "That is so cool. We're going to Washington!" Then, after a second, she said, "Well, at least *I'm* going to Washington."

"What's that supposed to mean?" Amy asked.

Tasha answered her with another question. "How do you think your mother's going to feel about this?"

Amy didn't respond right away. She knew what Tasha was implying. Other kids' mothers or fathers wouldn't have any problem agreeing to a school-sponsored trip. But Amy's mother was a little—actually, a *lot*—more cautious than other kids' parents.

She'd be particularly nervous about Amy's going to Washington, D.C.—for the same reason that Amy was so excited about going. The city where it had all begun could give Amy more understanding, more knowledge of herself. But it could also be one of the most dangerous places on earth for her to be.

Yes, there was definitely a possibility that her mother might object to the trip. She might even refuse to give Amy permission to go. But Amy suddenly had a bright idea, a way to get around any problems.

"What are you grinning about?" Tasha demanded.

"I was just thinking," Amy mused. "Don't they always ask parents to chaperone these trips?"

t2wo

"I can't believe I let my daughter talk me into this," Nancy Candler grumbled as she carefully folded a sweater on her bed.

Her friend and next-door neighbor, Monica Jackson, spoke from her perch on the edge of Nancy's dresser. "I would have thought you'd appreciate a free trip to D.C. Didn't you used to live there?"

"A million years ago," Nancy replied, placing the sweater in her suitcase.

"You must have some friends still there," Monica said.

"One or two," Nancy admitted. "We haven't really kept in touch. I haven't been back to Washington in thirteen years. I won't even be able to remember how to get around."

"Washington can be a lot of fun if you know where to hang out," Monica remarked. "There are a lot of great new restaurants. And I know some terrific jazz clubs."

"Monica, I'm chaperoning seventh-graders. I don't think I'll have much opportunity to hang out in any jazz clubs."

"You don't have to be with the kids every minute, do you? There are other chaperones, right?"

"Twenty adults are going," Nancy told her. "But even so, after a day of hitting all the sights with a bunch of twelve-year-olds, I don't think I'll be feeling up for any nightlife." She paused in her packing, trying to remember what the weather in Washington would be like at this time of year. Maybe she should bring a heavier sweater.

She didn't realize she'd been biting her nails until Monica brought it to her attention. "Are you nervous about this trip? How many kids will you be responsible for, anyway?"

"At least a hundred kids are going on the trip, but they'll be divided into groups of ten, and there are two adults for each group."

"That doesn't sound so bad," Monica said.

"No, it's not bad at all," Nancy agreed.

"Then why are you so tense?"

"I'm not tense," Nancy replied quickly, but she knew she didn't sound very convincing. She'd never been a good liar. Monica was right, she *was* nervous, but this didn't have anything to do with her chaperoning responsibilities. Now Monica was looking at her with undisguised curiosity, and Nancy was going to have to provide some sort of explanation.

"Going back to Washington . . . well, it's going to bring back a lot of memories."

Monica nodded understandingly. "Your husband."

"Yes. That was where we lived just after we were married. And before he was killed in the accident overseas."

"That must have been so tragic," Monica said sympathetically. "He never even got to see his daughter."

"That's right. He died before Amy was born."

She could see that Monica still bought that story. Amazing. Maybe Nancy was a better liar than she thought she was. Her husband hadn't died before his daughter was born. This so-called husband had never even existed. As for the real reason she was nervous about returning to D.C.—that was something Monica would never know.

After Monica had left, Nancy tried not to think about the impending trip, but she couldn't clear her head of the images. She only had to close her eyes to see herself, thirteen years younger, clinging to a strap on a crowded bus as it moved through the Georgetown neighborhood where she had lived. She was on her way home from work.

Nancy was tired. She was always tired at this time of day, and it wasn't because she'd been working too hard. Her job at the laboratory was pretty easy. She spent most of her days peering at slides under a microscope and then recording what she saw. It wasn't difficult, but it wasn't very interesting, either. If she was perfectly honest with herself, she had to say it was a completely boring job.

With all her university degrees in biology, she had always hoped she could work at an important job, doing scientific research that would make the world a better place, make people healthier, maybe even save some lives. Instead, she was working for a cosmetics company, testing the chemicals that went into the beauty products, making sure that the company's latest powder wouldn't make someone's nose fall off.

It wasn't what she wanted to be doing, but she needed the kind of money a job like this paid. Because she wasn't just supporting herself. She was taking care of Neil, her ten-year-old brother, too. Whenever she thought of him, she smiled—and then felt like crying at the same time.

She got off at her regular stop, went to the corner, and turned right onto the street where she lived. Lovely, stately old town houses lined the walk. Once, they had been grand homes for large families. Now most of them had been broken up into apartments. As she neared her own building, she saw her downstairs neighbor approaching from the opposite direction.

She couldn't see his face. As usual, he was lost in his daydreams and staring at the ground. But she'd recognize him anywhere by the straight, shaggy blond hair that always needed a cut and the battered violin case he carried under his arm.

"Calvin!" she called, and he looked up. He smiled and waved back at her. They met at the walkway that led to their front door.

"Hi, how was your day?" he asked.

"Fine," she said automatically, because that was what she always said, whether the day had been fine or not. "How was yours?"

As usual, Calvin's day had been much more interesting than hers. He worked as a tour guide, and he always had funny stories to tell about the out-of-towners he took around Washington.

"I had a bunch of Bulgarians today," he told her.

"When we got to the White House, a sanitation truck was coming out and they got all excited."

"Why?" Nancy asked.

"Don't know. They were speaking Bulgarian! Maybe they thought the President had just carried out his own trash bags."

Nancy grinned. "Or maybe they wanted to get some presidential garbage for souvenirs."

Calvin could always make her laugh. It was nice having him live downstairs. "C'mon up and have some coffee," she urged. "Neil would love to see you."

But Neil wasn't sitting in his rocking chair when they walked in. Only a gray-haired woman was there, watching TV.

"Hi, Mrs. Murray," Nancy greeted her. "Where's Neil?"

"He's sleeping," Mrs. Murray told her.

Nancy looked at her watch. "At six-thirty?" she asked in alarm. Neil sometimes took an early-afternoon nap, but he was always up at this hour.

Mrs. Murray nodded. "He was very tired."

Nancy went to Neil's bedroom and peeked inside. Curled up in his bed, her little brother seemed smaller than he really was, looking more like a five-year-old than a ten-year-old. But then again, even wide awake and standing up, Neil was too frail to look like a normal ten-year-old. The slight rise and fall of the blanket that covered him assured her that he was breathing, and she returned to the living room.

"Thank you, Mrs. Murray, I'll see you tomorrow," Nancy said, and the woman left. Calvin followed Nancy into the kitchen, where she began preparing coffee.

"Has Neil been to a doctor lately?" Calvin asked her.

Nancy smiled faintly. "He sees the doctor every week. Sometimes twice."

"But he doesn't seem to get any better," Calvin said. He wasn't being nosy, Nancy knew that. He was obviously truly concerned, so she answered him honestly.

"No, he's not any better," she told him. "He's never going to get any better, Calvin."

Calvin studied her seriously. "When did you find this out?"

"I've always known," she said simply. "I'm just finally getting to the point where I can talk about it." As if on cue, the tears sprang to her eyes. This was one of the reasons why she didn't like to talk about Neil—she always started crying. The other reason was the fact that she didn't want to accept what was going to happen to him. But Neil's doctor had told her she *should* talk about the situation. She had to prepare herself for what was inevitable.

She lifted the lid off the cookie jar and offered the

cookies to Calvin, but Calvin was more interested in learning more about Neil. "I know he's very sick," he said. "But you've never told me exactly what's wrong with him."

Nancy brought their coffees to the kitchen table, and they sat down. "He has a very rare genetic disorder. It has to do with the production of red blood cells, and—well, I won't go into details."

Calvin nodded. "I probably wouldn't understand the details anyway. But isn't there anything that can be done for him? Transfusions, transplants . . . there's so much happening today in medicine."

"There's a lot of research going on in genetics," Nancy agreed. "But there are still so many mysteries. Neil's condition . . . it evolved in the moment of reproduction. No one can say why." She swallowed hard. "Unfortunately, we know how it will end."

"He doesn't have much time," Calvin said. It was a statement, not a question, but Nancy answered anyway. Gripping her coffee cup tightly, she spoke.

"No. Not even a year."

Calvin reached out and placed a hand over hers. The gesture said more than words ever could.

After a moment of silence, he asked, "Does this illness run in your family?"

"Possibly," she said. "I don't know. I've been tested, and I'm not carrying the defective gene. As for my parents . . ." Her voice trailed off. Calvin waited, and finally, she explained.

"When Neil was diagnosed, shortly after he was born, my mother fell into a deep depression. I think she couldn't bear the thought of seeing her child die. She was in a hospital for years, and then I think she just willed herself to die. My father couldn't deal with any of this. He just took off. I heard he was killed in a car accident a couple of years ago."

Calvin let out a soft whistle. "I've known you for three years, and you've never told me any of this."

"I don't much like talking about myself," Nancy admitted. "And I'm getting tired of hearing my own voice now. Tell me something cheerful. Did you have any chance to make music today?"

"I entertained the Bulgarians at lunch, but I'm not sure how much they enjoyed it," he said. "I was pretty bad." He patted his violin case. Nancy knew that the violin inside was almost as shabby as the case.

Now it was her turn to be sympathetic. She knew that Calvin wasn't really into being a tour guide. His heart and soul were devoted to music. He aspired to be a great violinist.

"You weren't bad," Nancy told him. "It was the instrument. No one could make great music on that old fiddle."

Calvin sighed. "You know what breaks my heart? I could save and save for years and never have enough to buy a Stradivarius."

Nancy didn't know much about violins, but she knew that a Stradivarius was the finest violin ever made. Also the most expensive. A Stradivarius could cost more than a house.

"I'm sure there are other good types of violins," she said.

"Stradivarius is the best," Calvin said wistfully. "I read a story in the newspaper once about a struggling musician who was about to give up playing music. Then, one day, he was in a taxi and he found a Stradivarius someone had left behind. He knew how much it had to mean to that person, and he searched for the owner. He even took out ads in the newspaper. But no one ever claimed it, and he now owned a Stradivarius."

Nancy smiled. "Maybe that will happen to you."

Calvin sighed. "I never take taxis. Oh well, maybe I'll win the lottery." He shook his head. "Listen to me. Here I am, complaining about not having a fancy violin, when you've got a much bigger problem." He rose from the table. "Thanks for the coffee. Why don't you give me a call when Neil wakes up? Or just stamp on the floor. I'll come upstairs and play him a tune."

"He'd like that," Nancy said. "See you later."

After Calvin had left, she peeked in at Neil again to make sure he was still resting comfortably. Then she considered what she might make for dinner that would tempt him to eat. With his illness, he never had much of an appetite.

She was thinking about macaroni and cheese—Neil's favorite—when the phone rang.

"Hello?"

"Nancy Candler, please."

"Speaking."

"Nancy, this is Jim Jaleski. I hope you remember me."

"Dr. Jaleski! Of course I remember you." In her mind, she conjured up a picture of the noted physician, who had been one of her college instructors. It had been several years since she'd last seen him, and she wondered why he was calling her now.

He got right to the point. "I was just wondering if you might be interested in a new job."

"A job?"

"You were one of my best students," Dr. Jaleski said bluntly. "And I've just received a rather large grant to put together an exceptional team. It's a long-term program called Project Crescent."

"Project Crescent," Nancy repeated. She'd never heard of it. "What does the work entail?"

There was a moment of silence before Dr. Jaleski responded. "It's a top-secret program, Nancy, so I can't say much until I know you'll join the team. All I can tell you at this point is that it deals with genetic engineering."

Nancy gasped. This type of work fascinated her professionally—and personally, too. Genetic research was the only way to find a cure for people like Neil. "It sounds very interesting," she told Dr. Jaleski. "Can't you tell me anything more?"

Her former professor hesitated. When he spoke again, his voice was softer, almost as if he was afraid of being overheard.

"Nancy . . . what do you know about cloning?"

three

On their first full day in Washington, Amy's class had spent the morning touring the United States Capitol. It had been quite impressive, with all its statues and paintings and the beautiful landscaped grounds around it, and the tour guide had told them a lot of interesting stories. But so far, Amy's favorite sight was the one she was looking at right now. At the west end of the Mall, she gazed up in awe at the Lincoln Memorial.

"You know what's weird?" she told Tasha. "It looks so familiar! I feel like I've seen it before."

"You have," Tasha said. "Lots of times." She reached into her shoulder bag and pulled out a coin. Amy had never before noticed that every ordinary penny bore an engraving of the Lincoln Memorial.

The guide was pointing out the columns that surrounded the statue of Abraham Lincoln. "There are thirty-six columns," she told the group. "They represent the thirty-six states that made up the United States of America at the time Lincoln died. And above the frieze, you can see the names of forty-eight states. Those are the states that made up the union in 1922, when the memorial was dedicated."

"I always feel sorry for Alaska and Hawaii," Tasha murmured. "Sometimes people just think the connected states are America."

Justin Kelly overheard her. "Yeah," he grumbled. "That's why we're not exploring igloos instead of looking at ordinary statues."

But Amy didn't think this was any ordinary statue. "Lincoln looks so lifelike," she said. "Especially his face and his hands."

The guide nodded. "That's because the face and hands are based on actual castings of Lincoln that were made while he was president. You have good eyes," the guide added approvingly.

Amy couldn't deny that. At that very moment, she could see a tiny fly buzzing around the presidential head.

It landed on Lincoln's nose. Lincoln's hands seemed so real, she half expected them to bat the fly away.

The guide led them around to the side of the structure, where Lincoln's famous speech, the Gettysburg Address, was carved on the wall. Amy had read it before in a textbook, but reading it here made the words sound much more powerful. "I'll bet he was a wonderful person," she said aloud.

Carrie Nolan agreed. "Yeah, he was the kind of person who should have been cloned. It would be nice to have some Abraham Lincolns around now. Tasha, why are you making such a funny face?"

Amy glared at her best friend. Tasha recovered quickly. "Uh, I was just thinking, it's too bad they didn't have that kind of technology way back then."

The irony of the situation made Amy smile. She knew full well that it was right here that the first human beings had been cloned. Not on this very spot, of course, but right here in Washington, D.C. Which reminded her of something.

She sidled over to her mother, who was pointing something out to a couple of Amy's classmates. Amy waited until Nancy was finished and the classmates' attention had turned elsewhere.

"Mom, could we go see the place where you worked

on Project Crescent? Not the whole class, of course," she added hastily. "Just you and me."

"The laboratory's not there anymore," her mother said. "It burned down. You know that."

"But I'd still like to see where it used to be," Amy told her.

Her mother seemed to be looking past her. "I don't think we'll have time, Amy."

"Sure we will—there's lots of free time in the schedule. And I want to see where you used to live. It was in the Georgetown neighborhood, right? I saw it on the map. It's not far from here."

Nancy certainly didn't seem eager to explore her own past. "We'll see" was all she would say, and Amy could tell from the way she said it that this was no time to bug her for a definite answer.

The tourist guide was beckoning for the group to come closer to her. Amy joined her classmates.

"I hope you've enjoyed your visit to the Lincoln Memorial," the guide told them. "You'll be learning more about Abraham Lincoln when you visit Ford's Theatre, where a very important and very sad event took place. Ford's Theatre is where Abraham Lincoln was assassinated. I'll be leaving you now, and another guide will meet you there to tell you more about this great tragedy."

Amy's group piled into a bus. On the way to the theater, the driver pointed out an enormous monument off in the distance—a monument so tall that it seemed to loom over the city like a huge exclamation point.

"That's the Washington Monument," the driver told them. "You'll be going to the top of it later today, and from there you'll be able to see practically all of the city."

Amy hoped she could get her mother to point out the places from her past from there. Though she'd much rather see them close up. She really couldn't understand why her mother was still so reluctant to visit her old haunts. Amy shared her thoughts with Tasha, who was sitting next to her in the bus.

"I mean, I know all her memories aren't good ones. Her parents died here, and she had a brother who died too."

"That's pretty sad," Tasha said. "She was all alone."

"But she had friends," Amy assured her. "In fact, we're going to have lunch with one of them while we're here."

"It's cool to meet people who knew your parents before you were born," Tasha said. "Or in your case, before you were—what?—mixed in a test tube?"

"I'm not sure," Amy replied. "Maybe I was shaken in a bottle. Or heated up in a small pan over a Bunsen burner."

Their giggles must have carried, because the other parent who was with their group, Mr. Moore, turned around and spoke sternly. "Hey, you girls, stop laughing. We're going to a very serious place now."

The guide waiting for them in front of Ford's Theatre certainly looked serious. Or maybe a better description of him would be *sad*. His face was pale and thin. A cap pulled low over his straggly blond hair obscured his eyes, and his shoulders drooped. He smiled at the group, but it was a mechanical smile. When he spoke, his voice was dull, as if he'd been saying the same thing for years and the words meant nothing to him anymore.

"Good afternoon, and welcome to Ford's Theatre. It was here, on April 14, 1865, that a terrible event stunned the nation. President Abraham Lincoln was attending a play called *Our American Cousin* when a man by the name of John Wilkes Booth came into the balcony and—" He stopped speaking abruptly.

Amy knew who John Wilkes Booth was, and she assumed all her classmates did too. He was the man who killed Abraham Lincoln. But the guide didn't seem able to say it. Maybe he wasn't as bored with his job as he looked. Maybe he still got upset when he talked about the assassination.

But then, with her keen ears, Amy heard something

no one else could hear. Her mother drew in her breath sharply, as if she'd just seen a ghost. Amy didn't think the reaction had anything to do with Abraham Lincoln. Turning, she realized that her mother was almost as pale as the guide. And she was staring at him, which was odd. Nancy Candler was usually too polite to stare at people. But what was even weirder was the *way* she stared. *Hard.* Amy had never before seen her mother gaze at anyone so coldly, with a look so full of dark emotion.

The guide stared right back at her. He didn't look angry, though. He seemed upset and nervous. Finally he began to speak again. But this time his voice quavered.

"John Wilkes Booth shot Abraham Lincoln. The stricken president was carried to that house across the street, where he died the next morning. Now, if you will all please follow me . . ."

As they'd done during each tour, one parent went to the head of the group while the other brought up the rear. This time it was Nancy who took the lead. With her eyes focused straight ahead and her lips set in a thin line, she swept past the guide without speaking.

None of the other kids said anything, but Tasha knew Nancy Candler well enough to know something was wrong. "What's the matter with your mother?" she asked Amy.

"I'm not sure," Amy replied. "I've got a feeling she knows that guide."

"If she does, he'd better watch out," Tasha noted. "I don't think she likes him."

Amy agreed. All day her mother had been friendly with the guides, saying "please" and "thank you" and asking lots of questions. Now her mother was practically rude.

"Maybe he's an old boyfriend," Tasha suggested. "And he broke her heart."

Amy supposed that was possible. The man looked rather dreary, but he could have been handsome and outgoing long ago. If he *was* an old boyfriend, Nancy must have really loved him once.

Because it was very clear that right now, she hated him.

four

Sometimes it was impossible for Nancy to remember how bored she'd been at her old job, even though it had been only two months ago. Her working life had gone through a complete turnaround since she had joined Dr. Jaleski and Project Crescent.

On the last day at her old job, she had considered how much red dye could go into a lip gloss without turning the gook into a lethal weapon. On the first day of her new job, she considered chromosomes. At her old job, she had created cosmetics. Now she was creating *life*.

On this particular day, she checked the temperatures

in thirteen plastic containers. To a nonscientist this activity might not look like anything important. A layperson would never think that the contents of these containers could be human beings. But that was what the spongy material was, in a way. Inside the plastic boxes were cells, dividing and multiplying. They were the very beginnings of life. Out of this stuff would emerge female infants.

As Nancy adjusted a dial on the seventh container, she found herself speaking to the contents as if it was already a completely formed human being. "But you won't be any ordinary little girl. You're going to be somebody very special," she said.

Lost in her thoughts, she almost jumped at the voice behind her. "Is this a private conversation or can anyone join in?"

Nancy smiled at her boss. "I'm afraid it's just a one-sided conversation, Dr. J. She isn't answering me. Not yet, at least."

Dr. Jaleski laughed. "Even our little Amy, Number Seven, isn't *that* advanced."

That was how the team referred to the material developing in the containers. Amy, Number One; Amy, Number Two; and so on, up to Amy, Number Thirteen. It was kind of silly. The cells didn't need names—the numbers were enough for the scientists to keep track of each one. But one evening, when she and other members of the project had been out to dinner together and had been talking excitedly about their work, they'd decided that a name would make the cells feel more like people and less like "stuff." And since all thirteen of the girls-to-be were completely identical, they all got the same name. Nancy couldn't remember who had suggested Amy, but it turned out to be a name everyone liked. So now, whenever the scientists talked about their work, they would say things like "I'm running a test on Amy, Number Six," or "Let's check the DNA on Amy, Number Nine."

Now, examining the contents of this particular container, Nancy said, "I wonder how this one is going to evolve."

"Pretty much like all the others, I suspect," Dr. Jaleski said. "In most regards, at least. I think we're safe in assuming they'll all look alike, that they each will have the same level of intelligence and the same potential."

"True," Nancy said. "After all, each of them has the same genetic disposition toward athletic skills, musical talent, artistic ability, and all that. But what about their personalities? Their feelings and attitudes?"

"That's the mysterious part," Dr. Jaleski agreed. "We can't predict their emotional responses. Of course, their personalities will have a lot to do with the kind of people they become. So, while they might all have the potential to be, say, champion swimmers, only one of them might enjoy water sports. And she'll be the only one to win an Olympic medal."

"But they'll all be capable of winning," Nancy mused. "Or creating, or inventing, or doing anything better than anyone else."

"That's what we *think*," her boss cautioned her. "You have to remember that this is an experiment. There are no guarantees."

Nancy understood that. It was part of what made this job so exciting—not knowing how things would turn out.

Two months earlier, they had begun by taking DNA samples from volunteers, each of whom was superior in one way or another. The scientists attempted to identify which gene would direct the health of the subject, or the ability to organize, to learn, to retain information. And beyond that—the ability to sing on key, to jump high, to run fast, to see and hear extremely well. The genetic material had then been manipulated to bring it to a state of perfection, free of any impediment.

The samples were combined to form a prototype, and from that prototype, twelve duplicates were cloned so that there would be twelve identical organisms. Every day the organisms were examined and tested and studied, and every day there were new information to absorb, intriguing developments, even a few surprises. The biggest surprise occurred when the embryo of Number Twelve split into two. What had started out as an experiment with twelve clones became an experiment with thirteen.

And every day Nancy looked forward to going to work. She liked the people she worked with too. Dr. Jaleski was a kind and concerned director, more like a father to his staff than a boss, and everyone called him Jim or Dr. J. Practically every afternoon, he ate lunch in the staff lounge with Nancy and two of her colleagues, Dave Hopkins and Grace Morrison.

But on this particular afternoon, when Nancy came into the lounge, only Dave and Grace were there. "Where's Dr. J?" Nancy asked, sitting down at the table.

Dave peered at her with that dazed look he always wore. "He's not here?"

Nancy tried not to laugh. Dave was a brilliant doctor, but he was so intensely involved with his work, and his thoughts were so focused, that he never knew what was going on around him.

Grace, on the other hand, was aware of *everything*. She was just as smart as Dave, maybe even smarter, but her mind could take in whatever was going on. Older than Nancy, with a big reputation as an important scientist, Grace had become a role model for Nancy, and Nancy looked up to her. Grace had answers for all her questions, and she provided Nancy with an answer to the question she was asking now.

"Dr. J's meeting with Ferguson," she told Nancy.

"Who?"

"The accountant," Grace explained. "You know, that little man with the fuzzy hair who comes here every other week."

Nancy nodded. "Oh, right, I've seen him around." She always thought of him as Mr. Salt-and-Pepper because of his hair, black but sprinkled liberally with white. "I've wondered who he is."

"He's the financial watchdog," Grace explained. "Don't forget, we're being funded by a government agency, and they don't throw their funds around. So he's here to keep an eye on us and make sure we don't spend too much money. Jim's begging him for a budget increase today. He has a whole list of things we need."

Dave looked worried. "I hope he remembers to tell Ferguson we need to upgrade the computers. There's a new program available now that would help me get my data results in half the time."

Grace sighed. "Dave, it won't make any difference if

Dr. J remembers to tell him or not. The government's not going to give us any luxuries. We'll be lucky if we get enough test tubes."

The door of the lounge opened, and the janitor stuck his head in. "You folks mind if I empty the wastebaskets?"

"Come on in, Mr. Kendricks," Grace said.

"How are you folks today?" the man asked as he gathered the wastebaskets.

Nancy answered for them. "Just fine, Mr. Kendricks, how are you?"

"Not so good," the janitor told them. "My wife and I have been trying to adopt a baby, but all the adoption agencies say we're not eligible because I don't make enough money. I'm thinking about asking Dr. Jaleski for a raise."

"I wouldn't ask him today if I were you," Grace advised. "He's meeting with the accountant, and I don't think he's going to be in a very good mood."

Mr. Kendricks looked disappointed, but he thanked Dr. Morrison for the information and left.

Nancy gazed after him thoughtfully. "I wonder if he has any idea what we're actually doing here in the laboratory."

"I doubt it," Dave said. "And personally, I don't think the government understands what we're doing either, or we'd be getting more funding."

"They should understand that this is the kind of work that would win us the Nobel prize," Grace said wistfully.

Dave frowned at her. "*I'm* not doing this work so I can win prizes."

"None of us are," Nancy said quickly. She'd noticed that once in a while there seemed to be a little tension between Grace and Dave. Probably because Grace was a better-known scientist and doctor than Dave was.

Grace didn't pay any attention to Dave's comment. "The government probably thinks we're all mad scientists," she mused. "Creating monsters like Dr. Frankenstein."

"It's a shame," Dave said. "If they only understood how important our work is, they'd give us enough money to do it well. Our experiments could find a cure for spinal deformities, mental retardation, all disorders that have a genetic basis. With our findings, children could all be born in good health."

Nancy nodded. "Whenever I get frustrated or tired, I think of all the children who will survive, and all the lives that will be saved, because of the work we're doing. It keeps me going." Her eyes misted at the thought. There was so much they could learn from studying these genetically perfect clones, the Amys. If they understood how human life could develop perfectly, they could figure out how to prevent people from developing serious problems.

Sadly, the cures the scientists might discover would come too late for her brother. But maybe future children wouldn't have to suffer the way he did.

Lately, though, it seemed to her that Neil was feeling a little better. At least, he wasn't sleeping quite so much. In fact, when she got home that afternoon, he was awake and playing checkers with Mrs. Murray.

"Who's winning?" Nancy asked cheerfully as she plunked a bag of groceries down on the table.

"Not me," Mrs. Murray told her. "We've played three games and Neil's won them all. I'm so stupid."

"That's not true, Mrs. Murray," Neil said. "You just need to concentrate. Don't put your kings in a square where they can be jumped. But you're not stupid, no way. You make the best brownies in the whole wide world, and a stupid person couldn't do that."

Nancy pretended to pout. "Better brownies than I make?"

Neil looked torn. He could never bear to say anything negative about anyone. Then he brightened. "You make the best brownies with nuts, Nancy, and Mrs. Murray makes the best ones without nuts."

Nancy wanted to hug him, but she knew it would embarrass him in front of the housekeeper. "How are you feeling today, Neil?"

"Fine," Neil said. "Really good."

That wasn't true and Nancy knew it, but she also knew that Neil never complained. She couldn't deceive herself into thinking he was getting any better. There were a few good days among the many bad days, but there was no real change in his health and there never would be.

Just as Mrs. Murray was leaving, Calvin walked in. "Knock, knock," he called out.

Nancy laughed. "I'd invite you to come in, but you're already here. What's up?"

"Nothing much." He gave Neil a salute. "Hey, pal." Then he sniffed the air. "Something smells good."

"It must be my perfume," Nancy said, "because I haven't even started dinner. But if you're hinting for an invitation to stay and eat with us, you've got it."

Calvin winked at Neil. "Your sister can see right through me. I'm not expecting a free meal, though. I'm planning to pay for it." He pulled three cardboard stubs from his pocket. "Lottery tickets for everyone." He passed one to Neil and another to Nancy.

"Cool," Neil said. "If I win, I'll buy you that fancy violin you want, Calvin."

"Thanks," Calvin said. "But you might not have to do that. I'm feeling lucky this week."

"You say that every week," Nancy pointed out.

"I know," he admitted. "But this week I'm feeling *really* lucky." He kissed his own ticket and put it back in his pocket.

As Nancy went into the kitchen to make dinner, Calvin played a song on his violin for Neil. Nancy could hear it too, and she thought it was pretty. "Did you make that up?" she asked Calvin.

"Yeah," Calvin said. "Now I'm going to write some words to go with the music. Then I'll sell it to a rock star who'll record it, and I'll make a million dollars. Of course, I won't need a million dollars, because I'm going to win the lottery this week. But just in case I don't, it's nice to know there's another way to get a lot of money."

Neil laughed, and it was a lovely sound to Nancy's ears. On days like this—with her brother feeling better, with a job she loved, with a friend like Calvin—she felt pretty lucky too.

five

"Do we have to see another museum today?" Justin Kelly's face was screwed up into an expression that announced to the entire seventh grade his opinion of museums.

Max Barstow echoed his displeasure. "Yeah, can't we do something fun for a change?"

It was their third day in Washington. The day before, they'd gone to three art museums and a sculpture garden, and while the rest of the kids had enjoyed them, Max and Justin weren't exactly into cultural stuff. Today the entire group was going to the National Air and Space Museum.

"Can we all fit into the museum at the same time?" Amy wondered.

But she soon saw that this museum could have held the population of ten Parkside Middle Schools. It was huge, taking up three blocks. And once they were inside, no one complained, not even Justin and Max.

Paintings and statues weren't the highlights here. The galleries of the National Air and Space Museum told the story of aviation from its earliest days. Big models of famous aircraft hung from the ceiling. Kids could walk through a model of a space exploration rocket and go through the motions of flying a real plane.

At noon the group was going to have lunch in the museum's cafeteria. But Amy's mother presented her with an alternative. "Would you like to come with me to have lunch with one of the scientists from Project Crescent?"

Amy had met others who had worked on the project, but she didn't want to pass up the opportunity to talk to someone else who knew all about her. Outside the museum, she and her mother got into a taxi, and Nancy gave the driver directions.

As they traveled through a business district, she asked the driver to slow down. Quietly she asked Amy, "Do you see that parking lot over there?"

"Yes. Why?"

"That's where the laboratory was."

"*My* laboratory? Where I was—"

"Amy," Nancy warned her, with a meaningful glance at the taxi driver.

So Amy shut her mouth and looked. Only there really wasn't anything to see—just three levels of parked cars. It didn't look like the kind of place where anything important could ever have happened. No trace remained of the laboratory where the work of Project Crescent had taken place.

Amy knew that the lab had burned down. It wasn't as if she expected to see visions of the experiment, or the ghosts of people who had worked there. Still, it was kind of a disappointment.

"Can I see where you used to live?" she asked her mother.

"Maybe after lunch, if there's time."

The taxi dropped them off in front of a restaurant in the Georgetown neighborhood. Inside, the hostess approached them. "May I help you?"

"We're meeting someone," Nancy said, her eyes scanning the room. "There she is!" She waved, and Amy followed her into the dining area and toward a tall, attractive woman who had risen from a table.

"Nancy!" the woman called out.

"Grace!" The two women embraced. "It's so good to see you!"

"Yes, it's wonderful to see you, too," the woman said, but her eyes had left Nancy's face and were focused squarely on Amy's. "And *this*—this must be—"

"Yes," Nancy said. "Amy, this is Dr. Grace Morrison. Grace, this is Amy."

Dr. Morrison's eyes glowed like searchlights. "Number Seven," she breathed.

"How do you do, Dr. Morrison," Amy said politely. It was strange, just standing there while the woman looked her over. She felt like she was being examined by X-ray beams.

They all sat down, and a waiter brought them menus. Amy studied hers, but it wasn't easy to think about food while she could feel Dr. Morrison's eyes still studying her.

"This is amazing, absolutely amazing!" the doctor exclaimed. "You don't know how much I've wanted to see one of them. She looks perfect! Is she?"

"She *is*," Nancy said warmly, meaning more than what the doctor was asking.

"Does she have the mark on her shoulder?"

Amy knew Dr. Morrison was referring to the

crescent moon on her right shoulder blade. Nancy had explained to her that all the clones bore the same mark.

"Yes," Nancy said. "It came out this past year."

"Tell me everything," Dr. Morrison demanded. "Has her IQ been tested? What can she do?"

Amy shifted around uncomfortably in her seat. She was being talked about like an object. Or a dog that had been through obedience training. Was this woman waiting for her to sit up and beg? Fetch a newspaper?

Her mother picked up on her feelings. "Grace, Amy's a person," she said gently. "She's not something in a test tube. You can talk to her directly."

"I'm sorry," the older woman said immediately. "Forgive me, Amy, I'm getting carried away. It's just that you and the others . . . you were the center of my life at one time. And it broke my heart not to be able to watch you grow, to see how you turned out. We all worked so hard on you. Didn't we, Nancy?"

"Yes," Nancy said, and with a smile she added, "Now that Amy's almost a teenager, I'm working twice as hard!"

"We had such high hopes for Project Crescent." Dr. Morrison sighed. "And we ended up with nothing. What a shame that we had to terminate the experiment like that. It was such a waste."

"It wasn't a waste, not for *me*, Grace," Nancy said. "I came out of it with a wonderful daughter. And so did other people."

"Have you seen any of the others?" Dr. Morrison asked eagerly.

Fortunately, the waiter appeared to take their orders, and Amy didn't have to start telling stories about the other Amys she'd met, like the nasty actress or the racist ballet dancer. Or Aly Kendricks, the reject clone. By the time the waiter left, Nancy had turned the conversation to Amy's class trip.

"For most of the kids, this is their first time in Washington," she said. "So it's pretty exciting for them. We're trying to squeeze in all the major sights."

"I hope you'll fit me into your schedule," Dr. Morrison said. "I want to get to know Amy better. And spend more time with you, too, Nancy, of course. Tell me, what are you doing now? Besides raising your lovely daughter?"

Nancy told her about teaching at the university in Los Angeles. "You'll never guess who else is in L.A. now, Grace. Another member of our team—Dave Hopkins!"

"Really? What does he do there?"

"He's practicing medicine, working in the emergency room of a hospital."

"Oh, what a shame," Dr. Morrison said.

Amy was taken aback. "Why is that a shame?"

"He was such a fine researcher," the doctor told her. "Not always easy to get along with, but he had a brilliant mind."

Amy still didn't get it. It seemed to her that working in an emergency room, saving lives, was the perfect job for someone with a brilliant mind. Her mother tried to explain.

"What Grace is saying is that she's surprised Dr. Hopkins isn't doing something more—well, grander. Like what *she's* doing. Dr. Morrison travels all over the world, consulting with specialists and working with international medical organizations. I've been reading about your work in immune deficiencies, Grace. It's very exciting. You may just win that Nobel prize after all!"

Dr. Morrison shrugged. "I doubt it. So many people are working in that field now. I wish I could have continued with genetic engineering and cloning." She looked at Amy longingly, almost hungrily. "But there's so little funding available now. I suppose it's become too controversial."

Their food arrived, and as they ate, the conversation turned again to the sights and Washington. This was much more interesting for Amy. Dr. Morrison gave them some tips on places to go, and Amy began to feel a little more kindly toward her. As they parted, she didn't mind when her mother suggested that they all meet again during the week.

Walking down the pretty Georgetown street, Amy told Nancy her impressions of Dr. Morrison. "She's okay, I guess. Kind of intense."

"She's a very devoted scientist," Nancy told her. "She doesn't let anything get in the way of her work." She paused. "Amy . . . see that house? The one with the green shutters? That's where I lived. The shutters were white then."

Amy admired the stately building and tried to picture her mother looking out of one of the shuttered windows. "It's *big*."

"I didn't have the whole house," Nancy hastened to explain. "Just the middle floor. The owners were a lovely elderly couple who lived on top."

"Who lived on the first floor?" Amy asked.

Her mother stared at the house. "Amy, do you remember the guide at Ford's Theatre?"

"The man with the stringy blond hair? The one you were staring at?"

"He was my downstairs neighbor," Nancy told her.

"You're kidding! How come you didn't speak to him?"

Her mother's face took on the same grim look she'd had when she saw the guide. "It's a long story, honey, and it would bore you." She looked at her watch. "We have to get back to the museum." She hurried to the curb and waved her hand in the air. "Taxi!"

six

6

In the laboratory, the small plastic containers were gone. They had been replaced by thirteen incubators, similar to the kind that were used to hold premature infants in hospitals. Enclosed by protective glass, an Amy lay on a soft white cushion in each incubator. Each one had its own elaborate control board, with dials and lights and switches. These boards regulated the temperature and the humidity, and monitored each clone's respiration, brain waves, and movements.

Nancy was buttoning up her white lab coat as she entered the lab with Dr. Jaleski. She slipped the daily diary into her coat pocket so she could note any unusual occurrences, and the two began the early-morning rounds. They paused at the incubator of Amy, Number One, and gazed at the clone nestled in the sterile environment. The eyes were open and wide, and a tiny hand reached out as if she was trying to touch the glass.

"I hope they don't feel like they're in prisons," Nancy murmured.

"Have you heard any complaints?" Dr. Jaleski teased her.

"Very funny," Nancy retorted, but when she thought about it, she didn't think she would have been shocked if the clones had suddenly begun speaking. Every Amy was definitely more advanced than any normal infant would be at six months. They were larger and heavier and had more control of their arms and legs. If a normal infant was born at six months, she would be premature and have to struggle to survive. But according to the tests the scientists had run, these infants *could* survive outside of the incubator, and even thrive. The day before, two of the Amys had rolled over on their own, and if this development continued as all the other kinds of development had, by the end of this week they'd all be able to do that. They were all progressing at the same rate, within a few days of each other.

Except for one.

"How is Amy Thirteen coming along?" Dr. Jaleski wanted to know.

Nancy sighed. "She's the exception. I don't know what went wrong there. Physically she's in decent shape, better than an ordinary fetus, but she's not at the level of the others. Watch." She opened the lid of the incubator where Amy, Number One, lay and put her gloved finger inside. It hovered just within the range of the infant's vision. Immediately Amy's tiny hand grabbed it.

"Notice how she's able to focus on my finger," Nancy pointed out. "Her vision is remarkable."

"Impressive," Dr. Jaleski agreed. "Plus, she demonstrates an excellent reflex."

"They can all do that now," Nancy told him. "Except for Thirteen." He followed her to the last incubator, where Nancy raised the lid and put her finger inside. This clone didn't see her finger at first.

"She's not blind," Nancy assured him. "When I rest the finger just in front of her eyes, she sees it. Watch how her pupils contract." She demonstrated, and the infant's eyes did change slightly. This Amy didn't grab her finger, though.

"That's a normal response," Dr. Jaleski remarked.

Nancy nodded. "But she's not supposed to have normal responses. What's wrong with her?"

"We'll talk about it at today's meeting," Dr. Jaleski said. "I have to do some paperwork now."

Alone with the babies, Nancy went about the task of feeding them. Measuring each ingredient precisely, she mixed a very complicated formula. She took off her rubber gloves and replaced them with another sterile pair. She wished the babies could feel the warmth of a real human hand, but the scientists couldn't take any chances with possible bacterial contamination.

When each bottle was ready, she began feeding the Amys one at a time. When she opened the incubator of Amy, Number Seven, the clone raised both her hands, as if trying to take the bottle and hold it herself. Her hands were too small to wrap around the bottle, but the effort was what counted.

"That's a first!" Nancy exclaimed, and she noted the movement in the daily diary. "Good girl!" It was funny—she often found herself talking to this particular one, instead of just talking about her. She didn't know why—after all, this clone was no different from the others. Maybe she just liked the number seven.

Nancy's next couple of hours were taken up with conducting routine tests and entering her daily report into the computer files. Then she went down the hall to Dr. Jaleski's office, where meetings were held around a conference table. She was the first to arrive, and the janitor was still vacuuming the floor.

"I'll be out of here in a minute, Dr. Candler," Mr. Kendricks told her. "I got a late start this morning." He was looking tired and gloomy, and Nancy asked him if he was all right.

"The wife and I had another meeting with the adoption agency this morning," he told her. "Even with the pay increase I got, they're still saying our income isn't high enough. How rich does a person have to be to raise a child?"

Nancy sympathized with him. Personally, she too thought the agency was being overly strict with its rules and regulations. She knew that Mr. Kendricks was now making a pretty decent salary. She wondered if she herself would meet the incredibly high standards for adopting a child. Not that she was the least bit interested in doing that. Taking care of Neil was enough for her.

Just as Mr. Kendricks was leaving, Grace and Dave walked in. As usual, they were arguing.

"There has been absolutely no proof that vitamin therapies can have a positive effect," Dave was saying. "There are even studies that indicate the possibility of problems, like liver damage. I don't think we should expose the Amys to any risks."

"I disagree," Grace said. "We should take advantage of the fact that we have these subjects to experiment with."

Her words seemed to bother Dave, and he responded sharply. "They're not subjects, Grace. They're babies!"

Grace shook her head. "You are not thinking the way a true scientist should think, Dave. You're being too emotional."

Nancy stifled an urge to laugh. She'd never call Dave an emotional person. He wasn't someone who laughed or cried easily. He was so committed to his work, he didn't even have a private life. But apparently Grace was even more of a hard-core, practical scientist than he was.

Dr. Jaleski joined them, and the meeting began. Nancy began with her report on the condition of the clones. She took out her notes and told them about the progress she had witnessed that day. "Amys Number Four and Nine were able to grip my extended finger. Number Seven attempted to hold the feeding bottle herself. Her eyes reacted to light from a distance of twelve feet. Number Three responded to light flashes at ten feet. Brain wave patterns are typical of an infant of eleven months. Muscle control in the lower limbs has increased twenty percent. In two months, they should be able to stand and bear their own weight."

"Wow," Dave murmured. "Do you realize, if these babies were growing in the body of a mother, they'd be able to walk out of their wombs!"

Nancy smiled. "No, they would have made their desire to leave the womb long before now. But you're right, by the age of nine months, they should be walking."

"All of them?" Grace wanted to know.

Nancy hesitated. "Well, Number Thirteen may get a late start."

Grace spoke flatly. "Nancy, face it. Amy, Number Thirteen, is a dud. Now, I realize that sounds cold and cruel, but we have to look at the facts. She isn't on the same level, physically or mentally, as the others. What do the DNA tests reveal about her, Dave?"

Dave admitted that Amy, Number Thirteen, was not performing to the standards they'd come to expect of the clones. "And there are no unusual patterns in the DNA, unlike the others. I think we have to assume that there was some sort of breakdown in cell reproduction, or perhaps the prototype weakened when it split from Number Twelve.

Whatever the reason, her tests results reveal her to be an absolutely normal, if slightly premature, infant."

"So what are we going to do with her?" Grace asked. "She's already throwing off the statistics, and she could prove to be a fatal flaw in the entire experiment! Why don't we just get rid of her and adjust the figures so it will appear that only twelve subjects were cloned?"

"Grace, that's dishonest," Dr. Jaleski scolded her. "Scientists don't change their findings simply because the findings aren't what they want them to be."

"I know," Grace said. "You're right. I just don't want to see this entire experiment thrown out because of one loser."

Nancy winced. She had a lot of respect for Grace's genius. Still, she wished Grace wouldn't use a word like *loser* about the Amys. But if Nancy said anything, Grace would just tell her she was being too emotional and unscientific, like Dave.

"We don't have to make any decisions about Number Thirteen right now," Dr. Jaleski said. "But we do need to determine how the clones will best thrive once they're ready to leave the incubators."

"Can we arrange for them to live with families?" Nancy wondered aloud. "If we trained the parents, and if we were able to test the children weekly—"

"No," Grace said with determination. "That wouldn't work at all. No matter how educated or well trained the parents are, they would inevitably develop emotional ties with the children that would affect their upbringing. And what if the parents decided to produce siblings? That could completely disrupt the well-being of the clones. No, I say we keep the clones in a controlled environment, where we will be able to monitor them at all times and where they will be untouched and un-influenced by any outside sources or motivations or attitudes."

"Like love," Nancy murmured without thinking.

"What did you say?" Dr. Jaleski asked.

"Oh, nothing," Nancy said hastily, but from the way Dr. Jaleski was smiling, she felt pretty sure he had heard her.

Grace hadn't. She was looking at her watch and frown-ing. "I have to go. I've got a meeting with Ferguson."

Dr. Jaleski turned to her in surprise. "The accoun-tant? He's not here today."

"I know," Grace said. "I'm going to his office. If we're going to provide for a controlled environment for the clones, we have to get another budget increase so we can begin our preparations now."

Dr. Jaleski frowned. "I can bring that up with Fergu-son during his next scheduled visit to the lab."

"It certainly won't hurt for me to lay some ground-work," Grace said briskly. "Excuse me, everyone."

As soon as she had left the room, Dave practically exploded. "Who does she think she is? She's not in charge around here! Why are you letting her go meet Fergu-son on her own, Jim?"

Dr. Jaleski just shrugged. "I don't want to get involved in any power struggles. Besides, I trust Grace. She's as committed to Project Crescent as the rest of us. She won't do anything that could harm the experiment."

"I'm not so sure about that," Dave said grimly. "Do you mind if I take off? I'd like to join her at that meeting."

"Be my guest," Dr. Jaleski said. He turned to Nancy. "Do you want to go to the meeting too?"

"No thanks," Nancy said. "I'd rather feed my babies." That last word came out involuntarily, and she reddened with embarrassment. "I mean, the clones."

Dr. Jaleski walked with her to the laboratory room that held the incubators. "Are you feeling maternal toward the clones?" he asked.

"I guess it's inevitable," Nancy admitted. "I've got that maternal streak. I like to mother people."

"Like your brother, Neil," Dr. Jaleski said. "You take wonderful care of him. How's he doing these days?"

This wasn't a subject Nancy wanted to discuss. "Oh, he has his good days and his bad days," she said lightly. But she couldn't lie under Dr. Jaleski's penetrating gaze. "No, that's not true. They're almost all bad days now."

Dr. Jaleski knew about Neil's condition. He nodded

gravely. "Nancy, if there's anything I can do to help you out, you only need to ask."

"Thanks," Nancy said. His kindness only made the lump in her throat expand, and she was relieved to enter the lab where she could talk about the clones instead.

Dr. Jaleski stayed with her as she gave each feeding, making his own notes about the clones. When they reached Amy, Number Seven, Nancy pointed out how the infant was reaching to grab the bottle. And then the clone did something else.

"Dr. J, did you see that? She smiled at me!"

Dr. Jaleski didn't deny it. He made a note, speaking aloud as he wrote. "Facial muscles around the mouth reacted to the presence of project member Candler." He looked up. "Or maybe I should just write, 'Amy, Number Seven, smiled at Nancy.' "

That little smile made Nancy's day. Her mood was light as she went about the rest of her duties. A couple of hours later, walking down a hall, she saw Grace coming in from the parking lot.

"How was the meeting?" she asked.

Grace paused just long enough to give her a thumbs-up sign. "I'll tell you all about it later," she called out.

Clearly, whatever she'd learned about a budget

increase was positive, and that made Nancy feel even more cheerful. By the end of the workday, she was feeling so optimistic, she'd decided that somehow or other she'd get Neil to eat a decent meal that evening. And she'd invite Calvin to join them.

But she was almost out the front door when she heard her name on the lab intercom. "Nancy Candler, please report to Dr. Jaleski's office immediately."

It wasn't like Dr. Jaleski to keep them late. Worried, Nancy ran back down the hall and around the corner to the office.

Grace was already there, and she wasn't looking happy. "I've got things to do," she said. "Why do we have to have a meeting now? Why can't it wait until tomorrow?"

"I don't know," Dr. Jaleski said. "It's Dave who's demanding that we meet."

Dave walked in, carrying a folder in his hand.

"What's going on?" Grace asked.

Dave ignored her. To Dr. Jaleski he said, "What do you know about the agency that's funding Project Crescent?"

"Well, it's government sponsored," Dr. Jaleski replied. "But it's a new agency, and it doesn't have an official title. It's under the auspices of the International Science Institute."

"And do you have any idea what their goals are?" Dave asked.

Now Dr. Jaleski was looking a little irritated. "Of course I do. I can recite the goals and objectives of the project to you right now, if you want. Dave, what is this all about?"

Dave's tone was grim. "As I told you, I decided to join Grace in her meeting with Ferguson."

This was clearly news to Grace. "What? I didn't see you there."

"You were already behind closed doors with Ferguson when I arrived," Dave said. "So I decided to do a little snooping around."

Dr. Jaleski looked puzzled. "Why?"

"Well, to tell you the truth, it was because of Kendricks, the janitor," Dave told him. "The poor guy's having such a rough time with the adoption agencies, I thought that maybe it was his benefits package that kept him from qualifying. So I wanted to find his personnel file. Instead, I found this." He indicated the folder in his hand.

"Which is what?" Grace asked.

Dave opened it and read aloud. " 'Project Crescent. A proposal for the production of human clones created from designed and enhanced genetic materials.' "

"So?" Nancy asked. "That's what we're doing, isn't it?"

"That's not all. Listen to this." Dave continued to read. " 'Objective: To initiate the development of a physically and intellectually superior life-form. Goal: To establish a governing force for the entire human population of the earth.' "

He paused to let the words sink in. As the full force of what he was saying hit her, Nancy felt her entire body begin to shiver. It wasn't possible. It was too bizarre, too insane, too horrible to even contemplate.

Finally Dr. Jaleski spoke. His voice was dull, and flat, and full of despair.

"Ohmigod. We're creating a master race to take over the world."

seven

7

There were many times when Amy appreciated her superb physical condition, and this was one of them. Looking around at her classmates, who had gathered on the corner to wait for the buses, she saw exhaustion written all over their faces. They'd spent the morning doing the National Aquarium, the National Arboretum, and the National Gallery. They had walked and walked, and they had all pretty much overdosed on fish, plants, and art.

A lunch break had revived them briefly, but the tour of the Bureau of Engraving and Printing had practically done them in again. Amy, however, still had plenty of energy, and she was ready to hit the next important site, whatever it was.

"Where are we going now?" she asked Tasha.

Tasha made a great show of acting too exhausted to look at the schedule she carried. Amy took it out of her hands and read it herself.

"We're going to Arlington National Cemetery," Amy announced.

Tasha sighed. "Well, at least it will be quiet."

The buses appeared, and the students automatically divided themselves into three groups. Amy was supposed to go on bus number two, and so was her mother. But just as she was about to mount the steps, Nancy pulled her back.

"We're going on number three," she said.

"Why?" Amy asked. Then she looked up at the bus windows and saw the answer to her question. Calvin, the guide from Ford's Theatre, was in the front seat.

Once they were settled on bus number three, Amy confronted her mother again. "Okay, what's the deal between you and that guy? Was he your boyfriend?"

"No," Nancy said. "I told you, he was my neighbor. He lived downstairs."

"But what happened between you? Did you get into a fight? Did he throw wild parties in his apartment? Did he put *his* garbage in *your* trash can or something like that?"

"Amy, *please.*" Her mother's voice was getting testy. "This doesn't concern you."

That kind of statement had never stopped Amy from interfering with her mother's life before. "Mom, whatever happened, it was thirteen years ago! Get over it!"

Her mother didn't respond, and before Amy could go on, another chaperone approached them. He asked Amy to change seats with him so he could discuss some schedule changes with Nancy.

It was just as well. Amy could tell when her mother was immovable. She wasn't going to get any more information out of her now.

But there was another person who had to know the story. When the buses reached the parking lot for the cemetery, Amy got off before her mother and made her way over to the group that Calvin would be leading on the tour.

It was a long walk into the cemetery, and it wasn't as silent as Amy had expected. From off in the distance, the sharp report of gunfire made everyone jump and freeze.

"What was that?" Tasha cried out.

Calvin quickly reassured the group. "It's a gun salute,"

he said quietly. "There's a funeral going on." A moment later they heard the mournful sounds of a bugle playing taps. It put Amy in a solemn mood, and it must have had an effect on her classmates, too. No one had any difficulty remaining quiet.

Calvin took them to see the grave of President John F. Kennedy, and then they saw the memorial to the astronauts who had died in the explosion of the space shuttle *Challenger*. It was very moving, and Tasha shivered.

"It makes you think about how you never know what can happen," she murmured. "Life can be short."

"Yes," Amy said. "That's one reason why people should never hold grudges." She thought Calvin must have heard her. He looked at her sharply for a second.

The next stop was the Tomb of the Unknowns, where they watched the changing of the guard. "The soldiers will march twenty-one steps," Calvin told them. "Then they click their heels and face the tomb for twenty-one seconds."

It was an impressive sight. Of course, a couple of boys had to get obnoxious and start marching and clicking their heels in imitation of the soldiers. Tasha scolded them, while Amy took advantage of the distraction to scurry to the front of the group.

"Hi," she said to Calvin. "My name is Amy Candler. Nancy Candler is my mother."

Calvin smiled gently. "Hello, Amy." At that moment, Amy knew she wasn't telling him anything he didn't already know. Something in his eyes told her that he'd seen her before—and not just the other day at Ford's Theatre.

"You know me, don't you?" she asked.

He nodded. "But the last time I saw you, you were a lot smaller."

"You knew me when I was a baby?"

"I baby-sat for you," he told her.

Amy's eyes widened. "You did?"

"Just after your mother brought you home from the laboratory."

Now Amy was even more surprised. So few people knew about her origins. Clearly, Calvin and Nancy had been very close at one time.

"And you were my baby-sitter," she mused.

He nodded, but his small smile faded. "Not a very good baby-sitter, though."

"What do you mean?" Amy asked. "Did you drop me on my head or something? Is that why my mother isn't speaking to you?"

He looked straight ahead and didn't respond.

"It must have been something pretty bad," she pressed. "You guys had to be really good friends if you baby-sat me."

"We were neighbors," Calvin said.

"I know, you lived downstairs. You must have known my mother's brother, too."

That remark brought his smile back. "I certainly did. I used to visit Neil almost every day. I'd tell him funny stories about my tour groups and play him tunes I wrote on the violin."

"You play the violin?"

"I used to." He shook his head, as if to shake off the memory. "Your uncle Neil was a wonderful boy."

How strange . . . she'd never thought about her mother's brother as her uncle. But of course, that was what he would have been. It was then that she noticed the tear making its way down Calvin's cheek. Quickly he brushed it away.

"Calvin . . . my mother doesn't usually stay angry for a long time. I'm sure if you talked to her—"

But Calvin was shaking his head. "No, you don't understand, Amy. We didn't have an argument, and I didn't drop you on your head. It wasn't anything like that. It was . . . It was a betrayal."

He moved away quickly to catch up with a couple of kids who were wandering off. Amy stared after him, still hearing his voice. A *betrayal*. The word gave her goose bumps.

But her own words must have reached him in some way. Because later, back on the bus, he approached her with a folded paper. "Amy, would you please give this note to your mother?"

Amy nodded and took the paper from him.

"It's very personal."

Amy knew what Calvin was saying, and she tried not to be offended. After all, he didn't know how mature she was now. "I won't read it," she assured him. She put it away carefully in her bag.

The next stop on the day's tour was the Vietnam Veterans Memorial. The wall of black granite panels was inscribed with the names of the 58,000 American men and women who had died in that war, which had ended less than thirty years earlier. Amy approached her mother, who was staring at one of the names.

"I guess you remember when this war was going on, Mom."

Nancy nodded. "I found the name of someone I knew. The father of one of my best friends, back in elementary school. He was killed in this war."

"War is a terrible thing," Amy said. "All those people dying. If they could just talk about their problems instead of fighting . . . Or hating. I guess that's how it all starts, huh? One country is mad at another country, and no one forgives anyone else . . ."

"Amy." Her mother's voice was tired. "Please don't start asking me questions about my past."

"Okay. But I'm supposed to give you this." She fished the note out of her bag. "It's from Calvin."

At least her mother accepted the note. But she put it, still folded, in her own bag.

"Aren't you going to read it?" Amy asked her.

"Maybe some other time." And her mother moved off to round up some kids.

Well, Amy had done what she could, and she knew when to stop. She walked around the memorial, looking for Tasha. She finally found her, away from the others, talking to a man.

He was older, but with his scraggly beard and long hair, it was impossible to tell just how old. His clothes looked worn and grubby, too, and he was leaning on crutches. Amy wondered if he was asking for money.

Tasha introduced him to Amy.

"This is Mr. Mitchell," she said. "He was a soldier in the Vietnam War."

"You can call me Marty," he said.

"He was badly injured in the war," Tasha told her.

The man nodded. "Shot in the back. Both legs, too. I've been on these crutches for thirty years, and I'll never be off them."

Amy felt bad that she'd assumed he was a beggar. "Gee, that's awful."

"Yeah, I've had about ten operations, but none of them did any good."

Both girls were sympathetic. "You've suffered a lot for your country," Tasha said.

"No kidding." He waved a hand toward the wall. "Of course, these guys had it worse than me. Some of my best buddies are on this wall." He pointed. "See that name? I was with him when he was shot down."

Amy shuddered. "That's really sad."

"Yeah, it was. Do you want to see what he looked like?"

"Sure," Tasha said.

"I always carry a photo. It's in my car. I'm parked just over there."

Amy and Tasha exchanged looks, and Amy spoke for both of them. "We have to stay here."

"Aw, come on," the man wheedled. "Show some respect for a soldier who died to protect you. It's just a short walk. Don't you think my buddy deserves it?"

His voice was getting creepy. Both girls took a step backward. Then the man looked past them. "Forget it," he grumbled. "Lousy, ungrateful kids." He turned and started moving awfully fast for someone who needed crutches. And as he got farther away, Amy could see that he'd stopped using the crutches altogether. Clearly, he didn't need them.

"Amy, Tasha!"

The girls turned and saw Nancy waving to them. They hurried back toward her. "Who were you talking to?" Nancy asked.

Amy told her about the creepy man who'd claimed to be a wounded veteran of the Vietnam War, and how he had tried to lure them to his car. Nancy was upset.

"Amy, you know better than to talk to strangers!"

"We would never have gone off with him, Ms. Candler," Tasha assured her.

"Besides," Amy added, "I could have taken him on with one hand tied behind my back."

But that didn't calm her mother. Nancy lowered her voice, but it lost none of its intensity. "You don't know that, Amy. He might not have been an ordinary kidnapper. He could have been looking for *you*, personally!"

"I don't think so," Amy said doubtfully. "He was just as interested in getting Tasha to come with him as me."

Her mother wasn't pacified. "I'm going to find a police officer, and I want you girls to describe this man to him. And where was that tour guide? He should have been watching you!" Now she was getting even more agitated. "Unless maybe that man is connected to your guide. Maybe he told the man where you would be today."

"Mom!" Amy exclaimed. "Why would he do that?"

Her mother looked grim. "I'm going to find a police officer first. Then I'm going to find out who Calvin works for. And I'm going to see that he's immediately fired."

"Mom!" Amy cried out again in dismay. But her mother had already walked away.

e8ight

Over an hour after they'd been called into Dr. Jaleski's office for the emergency meeting, the scientists remained together at the conference table, talking, thinking, contemplating the unbelievable news that Dave had brought them. Nancy was still in a state of shock.

"Who *are* these people?" she wanted to know. "This organization that's behind Project Crescent—they can't be part of our own government."

"But the government is funding the project," Grace pointed out.

"Maybe the government doesn't know the real motives of the organization," Dave suggested.

"Or maybe they do," Dr. Jaleski said, and there was no mistaking the sadness in his voice. "Our own government isn't one unified, unanimous group with the same goals. For years we've heard rumors of secrets the government has kept from the people."

"Roswell," Dave murmured.

Dr. Jaleski nodded. "Exactly. It's possible that Project Crescent extends far beyond our own government. This organization could be part of an enormous international conspiracy that's infiltrating governments all over the world."

Grace considered this. "A worldwide conspiracy to create a master race. It's like something out of a science fiction movie. I suppose it *could* exist."

"But we're only working with female chromosomes," Nancy pointed out. "Thirteen genetically engineered girls can't create a race."

Dave offered a possibility. "There could be another project going on somewhere. At this very moment scientists might be working on the male counterparts to our Amys. They could be in the same situation that we've been in, operating in the dark, thinking they're going to find a cure for genetic disorders."

"That's true," Dr. Jaleski said. "And if there is an

experiment in male cloning going on somewhere, I feel certain those scientists can't know what they're doing, any more than we knew. No reputable scientist would agree to work on a project if the goal was world domination."

"It's an intriguing theory, though," Grace commented. "The two sets of clones, brought together at an age when they could begin to mate. It would be interesting to see what kind of offspring they would produce."

Nancy was shocked. "Grace! How can you even *think* about that?"

"I'm not saying that I *approve* of this," Grace told her. "But I'm a scientist. I can't help being curious."

"This is one case where curiosity could kill the cat," Dave said. "Just think of the terrible implications. Efforts to create a perfect race . . . why, it would be like the medical experiments in Nazi Germany."

"The potential consequences are beyond frightening," Dr. Jaleski agreed. "They're ghastly. The power this master race could have . . . the entire world could be thrown into an endless cycle of war and attempts at conquest."

"What are we going to do?" Nancy wondered aloud.

Dr. Jaleski responded immediately. "We're going to terminate the project."

His words were greeted with utter silence. Even if it was no surprise to the other scientists, his announcement was as devastating as Dave's news had been.

Their director continued. "We'll destroy everything. The donor identifications, the DNA charts, the genetic programs, the progress reports, the test results. All the data, all the equipment, everything."

"How?" Dave demanded.

"A massive explosion," Dr. Jaleski said. "We'll blow up the laboratory. And we'll do it in such a way that it will look like an accident, some sort of chemical reaction."

"What about the clones themselves?" Dave asked.

Nancy caught her breath and waited apprehensively for the answer. Dr. Jaleski rubbed his forehead. He looked like he was in real pain, and it was a few minutes before he spoke.

"The clones . . . they're the most dangerous evidence of all, and the greatest threat to world peace. As long as they exist, the organization would be able to carry out its terrible plans. As a scientist, I know they should be destroyed too. But as a humanitarian, an ethical person—I can't let that happen."

Nancy could have wept in relief.

Dave frowned. "I understand what you're saying and how you feel. But this *does* mean the organization will be able to use them to create their master race."

"Not if the organization can't find them," Dr. Jaleski said.

"What do you mean?" Grace asked. "How can we hide thirteen identical clones? They're small now, but they're going to grow. And they'll be noticeable."

"We'll separate them," Dr. Jaleski told her. "We'll have them adopted, placed in foster homes, orphanages. They'll be sent all over the world. Hopefully, they'll never meet, and they will never know how they were conceived."

Nancy looked at Dave, who was nodding. She nodded too.

But Grace didn't. "It's such a waste!" she cried out. "To take these exceptional life-forms and raise them as ordinary children—it's almost criminal! They'll never know how special they are. They'll never achieve their potential!"

Dr. Jaleski spoke heavily. "Grace, if the Amys know what they are, what they can do, then others will know too. And if the organization learns that they're alive, they'll be looking for them. They'll be able to realize their goals."

"How can we stop the organization from looking for them?" Dave asked him.

"By making them believe that the clones no longer exist, that they were destroyed in the explosion along with everything else." Dr. Jaleski looked around the table. "Well, what do you all think? Does anyone have a better idea?"

Nancy gazed at her colleagues. On their faces she saw the emotions she herself was feeling—sadness and frustration. But no one had a better suggestion.

"Could we at least mark them?" Grace asked wistfully. "Secretly, of course, and in a way that it would look like a birthmark. Then at least *we* could recognize them if we ever see them again. In the interests of science, they have to be identifiable."

"What's the point, Grace?" Dave asked. "Project Crescent is finished."

Dr. Jaleski rose. "I'll think about it. Now, if you have a computer at home, take some data with you and start erasing the disks. We'll meet back here at eight o'clock tomorrow morning. The project may be finished, but we have a lot of work to do."

Moving quickly, Nancy went back to her own office to pick up some disks. She was anxious to get home, to see Neil, to make dinner, to do anything but think about the termination of the project.

As she hurried through the parking lot, she saw Grace. The older woman was sitting behind the wheel of her car, but she wasn't starting the engine. She just sat there, staring into space, and even from a distance Nancy could see how depressed she looked. She went over to Grace's car and rapped on the window. Grace looked up and then rolled down the window.

"Are you all right?" Nancy asked.

Grace was more than depressed; she was angry. "I just hate this! All our hard work, all the effort we've put into those clones, and for what? We won't even see how they turn out!"

"I know," Nancy said. "It's hard to accept."

Grace sank back in her seat. "I feel so empty. Like it was all meaningless. Like the past eight months have meant nothing."

She was really in despair, Nancy thought. "Grace, would you like to come over to my place for dinner?" she asked impulsively. "I'm not promising to cheer you up, but it's better than being alone tonight."

Grace accepted the invitation. Nancy got back to the house first, and just as she was parking, she realized that she had nothing in the house to prepare for dinner. She'd been planning to stop at the market on the way home from work, but the emergency meeting had erased everything else from her head. She couldn't go to the market now; Grace would be here any minute. Running into the house, she pounded on Calvin's door.

"I've got a very important scientist coming for dinner and I've got nothing to serve!" she told him.

He grinned. "Calvin to the rescue. I just happen to have a fabulous spinach lasagna in my freezer. It's all yours."

"Oh, Calvin, how can I repay you?"

"Invite me to dinner," he replied.

It turned out to be a pleasant evening. Nancy opened a bottle of wine for the adults. Neil was having one of his less and less frequent good days—he actually ate a little lasagna, and he was the only one of the group who didn't do any complaining. Calvin played a new composition for them on his beat-up violin. When they all complimented him on it, he did his usual moaning and groaning about how much better it would have sounded on a Stradivarius. Grace let off steam by complaining about the end of Project Crescent and drank more than half the bottle of wine. Nancy worried out loud about finding a new job.

But Nancy was surprised at the way Grace talked about the project openly, in front of Calvin and Neil. The team had been sworn to secrecy when they were hired—they weren't supposed to tell a soul what they were actually doing—and now Grace was exposing everything. Neil was half asleep while Grace ranted on, but Calvin was floored when he learned of Nancy's work.

"You're creating clones? Far out! Hey, any chance I

could get a look at these Amys before you ship them off?"

"*No,*" Nancy said. "And you'd better forget you ever heard about this." Taking Grace aside, she gently reminded her about the importance of keeping quiet about the project.

Grace brushed that off. "Oh, what's the difference *now*? Who cares? It's over." From the way she was slurring her words, Nancy could see that Grace had had a little too much wine, and she made a mental note to call a taxi for her so Grace wouldn't try to drive home in that condition.

Nancy was disappointed about the outcome of the project too, but she wasn't devastated as Grace was. She comforted herself with the thought that maybe it would even be better for the little Amys to grow up as regular children in regular families, never knowing they were anything other than normal. Nancy was more worried right now about finding another job so she could support herself and Neil. She had difficulty sleeping that night, which turned out to be just as well, since Neil woke up in pain and she heard his soft whimper.

Sitting by his bedside, Nancy gave him some medicine and tried to comfort him with a story and a song.

But Neil must have sensed that there were other things on her mind.

"Are you worried about something, Nancy?" he asked in concern. "You look upset. What's wrong?"

She almost broke down and cried. Her dear little brother . . . so sick, and yet he still thought about other people and their feelings. She kissed his forehead, reassured him that all was well, and finally got him back to sleep.

As for herself, she was pretty groggy the next morning, but she managed to get to her eight o'clock meeting on time. Grace was a little late, but she behaved very professionally. Nancy didn't want to embarrass her, so she didn't mention Grace's behavior and loose tongue the night before.

"We need to set up a schedule," Dr. Jaleski told the scientists. "We need to work as fast as possible, but not so fast that we draw the attention of that accountant, Ferguson, or anyone else who happens to come around. I think we should start by finding adoption agencies where we can send the Amys. If we send off two or three a day, we can have them all out within a week. And that gives us enough time to plan for the explosion."

"Will we tell the agencies that the children are special in any way?" Nancy asked.

"No," Dr. Jaleski said. "We can't risk that. Hopefully, they'll thrive on normal baby care."

"I still think we should mark the Amys in some way," Grace continued. They all finally agreed to give each Amy a tiny tattoo, in the shape of a crescent moon, on the right shoulder blade. To anyone but the scientists, the moon would look like a freckle or a birthmark, nothing more.

They got to work. Although they thought the explosion would destroy all the materials, there was always the chance that a piece of crucial information might survive, so they erased as much data as they could. Adoption agencies were identified, and one by one the babies were picked up by delivery services and sent off to Europe, Australia, and Canada. One went to an adoption agency in New York, another to an agency in Iowa.

None of the scientists had any expertise in the area of explosives, but they managed to devise a makeshift bomb. It was set to go off at 5 A.M. on Saturday morning.

On Friday afternoon a messenger appeared to pick up a baby. Nancy went into the incubator room where the clones had been kept. Only two of the incubators were still occupied.

Nancy hovered between Amy, Number Six, and Amy, Number Seven. It didn't really matter which one she gave this messenger. Another messenger would be along in an hour to pick up the last one. But it was Number Seven that Nancy had felt a special bond with, and she wanted to put off losing her for as long as possible. So she picked up the baby who wore the bracelet that read "Amy, #6" and brought her out to the messenger.

Now it was almost over. The scientists gathered in Dr. Jaleski's office to wait for the last messenger, go over the checklist, and make sure everything had been done.

"Well, it's gone smoothly so far," Dr. Jaleski said. "In fact, Ferguson just called to remind me he'll be here on Tuesday for our regular budget meeting. So clearly, they don't know what we've been doing."

"When Ferguson shows up on Tuesday, all he'll find here is a pile of rubble," Nancy said.

"I'm sure he'll hear about it before then," Dave remarked. "It's going to be a big explosion. I'm sure it will be on the front page of tomorrow's newspaper."

"Can we leave now?" Grace said. "There's nothing more to do here."

"Well, someone needs to stay and wait for the last messenger," Dr. Jaleski said. He looked at his watch. "He should be here any—"

But no one could hear the rest of the sentence. Suddenly a huge roar tore through the air. The room immediately filled with smoke and intense heat, and the smell of fire was everywhere.

The scientists ran from the room and out the door into the parking lot. "What's happening?" Grace screamed.

No one needed to answer her. It was very clear what was happening. Something had gone wrong. The bomb had gone off precisely twelve hours early.

"Ohmigod," Dave said, his eyes wide as their laboratory became a huge ball of fire.

Nancy shrieked. "Number Seven! She's still in there!"

Dave grabbed her arm. "There's nothing we can do about her, Nancy. It's too late."

But Nancy broke free. She could hear the others crying, "No, Nancy, stop," but she ignored them. And she ran back into the blaze.

nine

Amy closed her eyes and pretended she was still sleeping in the hotel room she shared with her mother, but her ears were wide open. Nancy was on the phone with Dr. David Hopkins.

"The weather's been close to perfect," her mother was saying. "There's a nice light breeze and no humidity at all."

Amy had to concentrate a little harder to hear Dr. Hopkins's response coming from the other end of the phone. "No humidity? Are you sure you're in Washington, D.C.?"

"Yes, Dave, I'm really here. I'll send you a postcard of the White House to prove it to you."

"Are the kids driving you crazy?"

"No, not at all. We've packed the schedule with so many activities, they're all too exhausted to make any trouble."

It wasn't a very interesting conversation so far. But Amy perked up at Dave's next question. "Have you run into anyone from the old days?" Here was her mother's chance to bring up the subject of Calvin, and maybe she'd say something revealing about the past.

"Amy and I had lunch with Grace Morrison. She was very excited to finally see one of the—what was it she used to call the Amys?"

"Subjects, life-forms . . . Grace could never think of them as actual humans. Maybe because she herself wasn't very human."

"Oh, Dave, she's not that bad," Nancy said. "She just tries not to let her emotions get in the way of science."

"That woman *has* no emotions," Dave grumbled. "She's cold as ice. I never did like her."

"Maybe you're just jealous," Nancy teased. "She's a real big shot now, you know. And she must be rich. She's taking Amy and me to the most expensive restaurant in D.C. tonight."

Their conversation then turned to what Dave was up

to back in L.A., and Amy lost interest in any more eavesdropping. Was she ever going to be able to learn her mother's secret? What could Calvin have done to her? What had he meant when he said it had been a betrayal?

She might never find out. Her mother was trying to get Calvin fired from his job as a tour guide. She was convinced that the incident with the man at the Vietnam Veterans Memorial had been Calvin's fault. She had called both the police and the company Calvin worked for.

Amy had tried over and over again to tell her mother that she shouldn't blame Calvin. There were always slimy jerks hanging around public places. She and Tasha had made a stupid mistake by talking to a stranger. They both knew better than that, and if it was anyone's fault, it was their own. But her mother seemed determined to hold Calvin responsible.

When they went downstairs to the hotel restaurant, the entire seventh-grade group was having breakfast. Under threat of permanent detention, the students weren't treating the place as if it was the Parkside Middle School cafeteria; there were no food fights going on, and the conversations were quiet. Then Amy became aware of a buzz going through the room.

Tasha heard it too. "What's going on?" she asked.

Amy looked. A couple of police officers had just come into the room. She watched as the uniformed man and woman spoke to another chaperone. The chaperone pointed in the direction of their table.

Nancy was very pleased to see them. "Are you investigating the incident that occurred at the Wall yesterday? I'm sure the girls can give you a good description of the suspect."

"That won't be necessary, ma'am," the female officer said. She took a black-and-white photo from her pocket and placed it on their table. "Girls, is this the man who approached you yesterday?"

Amy and Tasha immediately identified the person in the picture as the man on crutches.

"He's a notorious scam artist," the policeman told Nancy. "He hangs out at the Wall and claims to be a disabled veteran. We picked him up last night."

Nancy wasn't satisfied. "But do you know what his motives were? Why did he pick my daughter?"

The police officers shrugged. "Because she was there," the woman said. "I doubt that he singled her out."

"Besides," Amy broke in, "he approached Tasha first."

"He goes after kids because they're more gullible and easier to steal from," the policeman said. "You girls were lucky to get away so easily. You shouldn't be talking to strangers."

He spoke sternly, and Amy and Tasha got the message. "We know," they chorused meekly.

The policewoman turned to Nancy. "The guy's just your run-of-the-mill common criminal, but we've got him now. Don't worry, he won't be bothering your daughter or anyone else again."

Nancy nodded. "Thank you for informing us."

As soon as the police officers were gone, she turned to her mother. "See, Mom? Calvin had nothing to do with it."

"Yes, I can see that," Nancy said. "I was wrong. Excuse me."

When she left the table, Amy said, "I hope Calvin hasn't already been fired. I'd feel terrible."

"Me too," Tasha agreed. "He's nice. And he seems kind of sad. Like he's lost or something."

Amy knew exactly what Tasha meant. She noticed that her mother had left her handbag behind on the chair where she'd been sitting. Amy looked around to make sure Nancy wasn't on her way back to the table. Then, furtively, she opened the bag and peeked inside.

The folded note from Calvin was still there. At least Nancy hadn't thrown it away. But it didn't look like it had been unfolded. Too bad Amy's talents didn't include X-ray vision, so she could "accidentally" read the contents. Her morals kept her from actually unfolding the note and looking at it.

She was happy to see that her mother had morals too. Apparently she'd been able to withdraw her complaint about Calvin, because the guide reappeared on one of their buses that morning.

The group had another full day of activities. They went on a tour of the White House, and although the guide had warned them that they wouldn't be running into the President, Amy couldn't help hoping. When he never appeared, she wasn't all that disappointed. After all, what would she have said to him anyway? "Mr. President, could you please increase federal funding for cloning research?" Her mother would have killed her.

After the White House, there were more museums, a sculpture garden, the Pentagon, and memorials to more Presidents. It was all pretty interesting, but Amy was more intrigued with watching for any interaction between her mother and Calvin. Or seeing if she could read anything in their faces. Would Calvin be angry that Nancy had tried to get him fired? Would he be grateful for getting his job back?

These remained unanswered questions. Nancy and Calvin had no contact at all.

She wasn't really looking forward to dinner that night with her mother's old colleague Grace. Even if the restaurant was amazingly good, she wouldn't be able to enjoy her meal if Grace kept staring at her as if she was some freak.

But Amy had to admit, the place Grace brought them to was the fanciest restaurant she had ever seen. There was elaborate gilded molding around the windows and old-fashioned paintings in gold frames on the walls, and the tables glittered with all the silver and crystal on them. There were flowers, candles, and soft music, and the waiters wore tuxedos. Amy was grateful that her mother had made her change her jeans. All the other diners were very dressed up.

Grace pointed out the well-known people. There were senators, and ambassadors, and a woman Amy recognized from the news on TV. One of the tuxedoed waiters appeared with a smile and handed them huge menus. Everything on the menu was written in French.

"I could ask the waiter to translate for us," Grace offered.

"That won't be necessary," Nancy said, with more than a little pride in her voice. "Amy reads French very well."

Grace looked at Amy with interest. "How did you learn French, Amy?" she asked. "Did you simply open a French dictionary and read through it?"

"No," Amy said. "I'm taking French at school. This is my second year."

"At school?" Grace repeated. "What kind of school?"

"Just a regular public middle school," Nancy told her.

Grace was surprised. "But, Nancy, surely Amy doesn't need to be taught in an ordinary way. She should be tutored by the world's greatest minds!"

"No thanks," Amy said quickly, hoping her mother wouldn't get any crazy ideas. "I like regular school."

Grace ignored her. "Nancy, I don't think you have any idea at all what Amy's capable of doing!"

Nancy replied patiently. "Amy's in perfect health, Grace. All her senses are unusually acute. She excels in physical activities, she can learn and memorize easily, and she's brighter than other kids her age. I know this."

"But how much brighter?" Grace pressed her. She actually spoke to Amy. "Amy, I'm going to recite a list of numbers. I want you to add them in your head, and I'm going to time your response."

"No," Nancy said sharply. "Grace, we've been through this already. She's not here to be examined."

Grace was looking extremely frustrated now. "Nancy, you haven't had her measured or tested or evaluated or—"

"That's right," Nancy interrupted. "And I have no intention of doing any of that."

"But it's your responsibility as a scientist!"

"No, Grace," Nancy responded. "I have a greater responsibility. As a mother. Now, can we please change the subject?"

Grace was clearly reluctant, but she obliged. "Tomorrow is your last full day here, isn't it? What are you planning to do?"

"We're taking the kids to tour the FBI headquarters," Nancy told her. "After that, we're having a picnic by the Potomac River."

Grace nodded. "How nice," she said, but she didn't seem terribly interested. The waiter appeared then to take their orders, and afterward Nancy excused herself to go to the rest room.

Clearly, Grace couldn't pass up one more chance to test the subject sitting across from her. "Amy, do you see the woman in the yellow dress, with the man in the gray suit, way over by the window? They're both Supreme Court justices! Can you hear what they're saying to each other?"

Amy rolled her eyes, but she turned her head slightly to face the couple in question, and she concentrated. A few seconds later, she turned back to Grace.

"Yes, I can hear them."

"What are they talking about?" Grace asked excitedly.

Amy recited the few seconds of conversation she'd picked up. "The man asked the woman if it's supposed to rain tomorrow. The woman said she didn't think so but hadn't seen a weather report. Then the man said he's hoping it's nice tomorrow, because he promised the kids he'd go on a bike ride with them. The woman said that sounded like fun."

It wasn't very thrilling, but Grace seemed pleased. And Amy felt like she'd just thrown a dog a bone.

ten 10

As Nancy raced back to the laboratory, she could see that there would be no need to open any doors. The explosion had shattered all the glass in the front of the building, and what had once been a wide door was now a gaping hole in the wall. Leaping over the bricks and shards of glass, she found herself in the hall and turned toward the room where the clones had been kept in their incubators.

Her vision was cloudy. The hall was filled with gray smoke, and it got thicker as she neared the big room. The floor was littered with debris, and she tripped twice. At one point she fell down and felt something slice her knee, but she couldn't see whether she was bleeding. It wouldn't have made any difference anyway. She had to keep moving; she had to get to the room. Her mind was racing, out of control, and her heart was pounding wildly. She had no idea what she would find in that room. Melted incubators, maybe. And the charred remains of one cloned infant . . .

The heavy smoke made it almost impossible to see. And when she was finally able to make out the entrance to the room, she didn't even know whether she'd be able to get inside. A huge, thick beam had fallen, blocking her way. There was a lot of rubble too, creating a mountain at least six feet high. She couldn't see the condition of the room beyond the mess.

She pulled at the rubble, which was still hot, and burned her fingers. But she managed to get close enough to the beam so that she could climb over it. In the process, she cut her arm on something and experienced a thud as a dangling chunk of the remaining piece of the door hit her head. She was momentarily stunned— but not so dazed that she didn't realize how hot it was getting.

The heat became more intense. Once she'd clambered over the rubble, she could see why. A red-orange wall of fire blocked her view of the incubators.

Despite her panic, she tried to think calmly and

clearly. There was no way she could break through that wall of fire without severely injuring, maybe even killing herself. But maybe she could get around it.

Facing the blaze, she stumbled and groped along the wall until she made out a small break in the curtain of flames. By now she was coughing and barely able to breathe, but something inside her kept her going, and she edged into the space. She could make out the glass incubators now, and they appeared to be intact. Even so, her heart was in her throat. What would she find inside the seventh one? Would she be too late to rescue the last remaining Amy?

The glass forms were swimming before her eyes. She counted to the seventh one and started toward it. But even when she was looking down on it, she couldn't see through the glass. It was covered in a thick layer of ash. At least it appeared to be in one piece, and she forced it open.

The little form inside was so still . . . but then the lashes fluttered and big brown eyes looked directly up at her. The tiny rosebud mouth puckered, then opened, and issued a shrill baby wail. Nancy had never heard a sweeter sound.

She gathered Amy, Number Seven, into her arms. Clutching the baby tightly, she made her way back through the break in the flames, over the beam and the rubble, and back into the smoke-filled hall. It was even darker now. She had to hold the baby with one arm and feel her way against the wall with her other hand. She half-ran, half-stumbled back down the hall and prayed that her sense of direction had remained intact. Finally she saw a hint of natural light. Just a few more steps in that direction, and she broke free from the inferno into the safety outdoors.

It was chaos and confusion out there. Dazed and exhausted, she was dimly aware of the noise, people shrieking and yelling, the drone of a helicopter directly overhead, the scream of fast-approaching sirens. Firefighters dragging an enormous hose raced by without even seeing her. Then Dr. Jaleski was by her side.

"Are you all right?" he asked anxiously.

"Yes," she replied breathlessly, "and I think the baby is okay too."

"Get her out of here," he said. "The police are on their way, and that means the television cameras and reporters, too. We don't want any questions."

Nancy nodded and started toward the parking lot. Fortunately, in all the confusion, no one paid any attention to a bedraggled woman in a white lab coat carrying a baby to a car. Nancy was dizzy from the smoke, she was in pain from cuts and burns, and she was still in a state of panic, but somehow she managed to get herself and Amy, Number Seven, back to the house in Georgetown.

Thank goodness Neil was sleeping when she staggered into the apartment. He would have been so upset by her condition. It was hard enough explaining her appearance to Mrs. Murray, but she made up something about a friend's house burning, the friend being taken away in an ambulance, the friend's baby left to be cared for by Nancy. She called Calvin and sent him out for baby bottles and diapers. Fortunately, he was a good enough friend to hear the urgency in her voice and not waste time asking questions. And then she collapsed.

Never in her life had she experienced such a trauma, and she hoped with all her heart and soul that she would never go through anything like it again. But it was amazing how resilient the human body could be. Only a couple of hours later, cleaned up and with bandages on all her superficial cuts and wounds, she was feeling almost normal. Neil lay on the sofa, watching her in wonderment while she fed the baby. From the kitchen came the rattle of pots and pans as Calvin threw something together for their dinner.

"She's pretty," Neil whispered. Nancy held the baby closer to him so he could stroke the downy softness of the baby's hair and inhale the sweet baby smell. He seemed particularly weak that day, but he wasn't in any pain, and the surprise of the baby had brought a special light to his eyes.

Calvin joined them. "I am pleased to announce that there is a delicious chicken pot pie in the oven," he said.

"That sounds wonderful," Nancy said appreciatively. "What do you think, Neil? You like chicken pot pie."

Her brother managed a small nod, but Nancy had a feeling he wasn't going to have much of an appetite that evening. He really did seem unusually tired and listless.

Calvin gazed down at the baby. "What about you, little one? Are you going to eat the delicious dinner I've prepared?"

Nancy smiled. "I'm sure she'd love your chicken pot pie, Calvin, but I'm afraid she doesn't have the teeth to eat it with."

Calvin faked a look of disappointment. "But she's supposed to be so mature for her age!" He sat down on Nancy's other side. "How old *is* she, anyway?"

"I'm not sure," Nancy said. "I mean, I don't know what should be considered her date of birth. The eggs were fertilized eight months ago, but if this had happened in the womb, she probably wouldn't even be born yet."

The bottle's nipple had slipped out from between the

baby's lips, and she let out a howl. Hastily Nancy got the bottle back into position.

"Well, she's definitely born now," Calvin commented.

"Then this should be her birthday," Neil suggested. "Today. Now."

Nancy didn't think this would be her decision to make, but she smiled at her brother. "Okay." She looked at the baby. "Happy birthday, Amy!"

"Can we keep her?" Neil asked.

Nancy hesitated. "Well, she'll be staying with us for a while, I think. But she needs a family, Neil."

"We can be her family," Neil said, and it dawned on Nancy that his voice was becoming increasingly soft.

"Let's watch the news on TV and see if there's anything about the explosion," Nancy said. Calvin served dinner, and they ate in front of the television. At least, Nancy and Calvin ate. Neil didn't touch his chicken pie. Nancy kept a concerned eye on him while she checked out the images on the TV screen.

The anchorman spoke solemnly. "At four o'clock this afternoon, an explosion of unknown origin rocked a scientific laboratory in southwest Washington. Our reporter is at the scene."

The serious face of a woman filled the screen. "It took firefighters three hours to extinguish the flames. What was once a noted private scientific institution, home of many significant government experiments, is now a large pile of smoldering rubble."

The camera panned back, and Nancy couldn't contain a gasp. Had she actually gone into that place just three hours before? It was hard to believe that an actual building had ever stood there, amid the debris and the blackened earth. Exhausted-looking firefighters with blackened faces were trudging away, and in the distance, she could see a police officer talking to Grace. Nancy knew they could count on Grace's professional discretion to withhold anything really significant about their work.

The reporter continued. "This is Dr. James Jaleski, director of an ongoing project in the laboratory. Dr. Jaleski, do you have any idea what could have caused the explosion?"

Nancy's boss was pale but composed. "No, there are a variety of possible explanations, including the fact that there were many chemicals in use. The explosion could have resulted from an unexpected reaction. I don't think we'll ever know for sure."

"Is there no possibility of foul play?" the reporter asked.

Dr. Jaleski looked startled. "Why do you ask that?"

"Well, Doctor, I'm sure you are aware that there have always been rumors about this laboratory and its use as a place where secret government experiments have been conducted."

"No," Dr. Jaleski said. "I wasn't aware of that."

"But isn't it true, Doctor, that the scientific investigation currently in progress was related in some way to cloning?"

Dr. Jaleski was trying to control the shock he must have been feeling. It was amazing how the media could ferret out the deepest and darkest secrets.

Nancy could almost see his mind working. He couldn't tell the truth, of course. But if he denied this completely, the reporter would press him for information as to what the project had been all about. And perhaps he should use this forum to get a message across to the real powers behind Project Crescent.

He chose his words very carefully. "It is true that some tests were being conducted to determine the potential implications of the cloning process."

The reporter didn't mess around. "Were people being cloned in this laboratory, Doctor?"

"Some effort was being made at the replication of very basic life-forms," Dr. Jaleski acknowledged. "I believe that we may have been on the verge of some sort of scientific breakthrough. Unfortunately, all materials associated with the experiments have been completely destroyed."

"Including the life-forms?" the reporter asked.

"Yes. Including the life-forms."

Nancy heard no more. She was suddenly distracted by an ominous noise—a wheezing sound that her little brother was making.

"Neil? What's wrong?"

Neil didn't answer. His eyes were open, but he was staring blankly, and there was no expression on his face. His body was shaking.

Hurriedly Calvin took the baby from Nancy's arms so she could rush to her brother's side. "Neil? Neil! Look at me! Neil!" Nancy yelled.

But Neil didn't respond, and the shaking increased. His whole body appeared to be racked with involuntary movement.

"He's having convulsions!" Nancy cried out. "Calvin, call 911, get an ambulance! No, it'll take too long. I'll drive him to the hospital. Watch the baby!"

Her brother was no infant, but the disease had wasted his poor, frail body, and he was almost as light as Amy, Number Seven. Nancy gathered him in her arms and ran out the door.

eleven

"What bus are you on today?" Amy asked Tasha the next morning as they were waiting in the hotel lobby.

"Number one. What about you?"

"I'm on two."

Tasha surveyed her classmates. "Maybe I can trade with someone."

"No," Amy said. "Trade with me."

"Why?"

Amy lowered her voice. "Because my mother's a chaperone on number two. And I don't want her watching me while we're in the FBI building." She glanced around furtively to make sure she couldn't be overheard. "I'm going to try to get away from the group and do a little exploring on my own."

Tasha's forehead puckered. "What for?"

"C'mon, Tasha, *think.* You watch *The X-Files.*"

Tasha's face took on that I'm-so-much-more-mature-than-you expression. "Amy, I hate to break it to you, but Fox Mulder is a character. He's not a real person, and you're not going to find him hanging out in the FBI building."

Amy produced an equally condescending face. "I *know* that, Tasha. But there might be some real X-files. Maybe they're not *called* X-files, but I'll bet that somewhere in that building, there's information about Project Crescent."

"Oh, give me a break," Tasha groaned. "Do you have any idea what kind of security there's going to be in the J. Edgar Hoover FBI Building? There's no way you'll be able to go off on your own, and you know it. Now tell me the real reason why you want to be on bus number one."

Amy relented and told the truth. "Because Calvin's on that bus. I can see him from here. This might be the last time I see him, so it could be my last chance to talk to him. I've got to find out what happened with my mother."

112

Being a true best friend, Tasha didn't quiz Amy any further and exchanged bus tickets. Amy took off. Passing her mother, she called out, "I'm on one, Mom," and hurried away before her mother could suggest she change.

As she boarded the first bus, she noticed that there was no one in the driver's seat. As soon as all the students were seated, Calvin made an announcement.

"Kids, the driver assigned to this bus has been taken ill. The company can't send a replacement over right away, so I'll be doing double duty, as driver and guide. Don't worry, I'm fully qualified and licensed to drive a bus."

Amy wasn't worried, and no one else looked concerned either. Nonetheless, Amy was very glad that her mother wasn't hearing this. If she didn't trust Calvin as a guide, she certainly wouldn't think too highly of him as a driver.

She soon realized that her mother would have nothing to worry about. In the thick of the morning rush hour, Calvin drove skillfully, with care and caution. He maneuvered the big bus smoothly through the traffic, slowly and steadily, until they turned onto less congested roads and he could go a little faster. His reactions were quick too, as they discovered before too long. Calvin had just turned onto a road leading to the highway entrance when, out of nowhere, a figure darted into the road in front of the bus. Calvin swerved and slammed on the brakes.

It wasn't a terrible jolt, so no one screamed. But when she looked out the window, Amy couldn't see the person who had run in front of the bus, and she was afraid he or she might now be under it.

Calvin too was clearly concerned. He turned around and looked at them. "Everyone okay?" he asked. Assured that no one had banged their head, he pulled on the lever that opened the bus door, jumped down from his seat, and ran out. Several students rushed to look out the windows.

"Can you see anything?" someone yelled.

Someone else yelled back, "The guy's getting up, he must be okay." A moment later, Calvin was mounting the stairs to the bus with the man following closely behind. Most of the kids were looking at the man, who was dressed strangely for a spring day, with a scarf wrapped around the lower part of his face and large sunglasses hiding the upper part. Or maybe they just wanted to see if he was limping or bleeding.

But Amy couldn't keep her eyes off Calvin. He'd always looked kind of pale, but now he was completely white. And, as it turned out, for good reason.

He spoke steadily, but there was a definite strain in his voice. "Kids, you'd better do what this man says."

The man stepped back a little, and now everyone could see the gun in his hand. Amy heard a gasp, then a shriek, but when the man yelled "Shut up," everyone did.

"Which one of you is Amy Candler?" he demanded.

There was no way Amy could deny her identity—half the occupants of the bus turned and looked directly at her.

"Okay," the man said. "The rest of you, off the bus."

When nobody moved, the man repeated his command more emphatically. "Off the bus! Or I start shooting."

There was a dead silence as the students rose from their seats and moved into the aisle. Amy could have sworn she heard dozens of hearts thumping simultaneously. Or maybe it was just her own. She willed herself to stay calm and alert as the bus emptied out. Finally there was no one left but the man with the gun, Calvin, and Amy.

The man kept the gun aimed at Calvin's head. "Okay. Close the door and start driving. I'll give you directions."

"No."

"What did you say?"

"I'm not putting this child's life at risk," Calvin said. "You'll have to shoot me."

But the man didn't pull the trigger. Instead, he backed up a few steps until he was in the aisle alongside Amy. Then he grabbed her by the arm and pulled her up. Now the gun was pointed at *her* head.

"How would you like to see this kid's brains splattered all over the bus?" he asked. "Now, drive."

Calvin had no choice. He had to obey. Sitting in the driver's seat, he jerked the lever to close the door and started the engine.

Amy was amazed to find that she still had the power to speak. "Who are you? What do you want?"

"You," he said.

Alarm bells went off in her head. He had to be from the organization. Somehow, they'd found out she was in Washington. They'd probably been watching her for days, just waiting for the right moment to grab her.

She tried to think. Was she strong enough, fast enough, to get the gun out of the man's hand? No, this guy was big—and he acted like a professional. He'd probably been hired by the organization for just this purpose, and they wouldn't have hired someone who couldn't handle her strength.

Her mind was racing as she tried to come up with

other options. But there weren't any. Then she realized it wasn't only her mind that was racing—the bus had picked up speed too. Dangerous speed, going faster and faster.

"Hey, you!" the man yelled to Calvin. "Slow down!"

But this time Calvin didn't obey.

twelve 12

Nancy knew that the doctor was speaking to her. She could hear him. She even understood what he was saying. Yet the words seemed to be floating over her head and hanging in space, as if no one was available to accept them.

"We're very sorry," the doctor was saying. "You must believe us, we tried everything, but there was nothing we could do to save him."

"I believe you," she said automatically. She wondered why he was using words like *us* and *we* when it was only him standing there, talking to her, in the waiting area of the hospital emergency room. Strange, she thought, how when you're faced with a tragedy, your mind focuses in on silly little details like this. He was probably referring to the nurses and the other doctors who had all tried to help Neil.

It really didn't matter what words the doctor used. It didn't change the truth of the matter. Her little brother, Neil, was gone forever.

She tried to focus on what the doctor was saying. "Is there anything we can do for you?" he was asking her. "Can we call someone? A family member? A friend?"

"No, thank you," Nancy said. Because there was no one to call. Now that Neil was gone, she had no family members. As for friends . . . she didn't want to bother any of her colleagues, after their traumatic day at work. And her only other friend was in her apartment, taking care of Amy, Number Seven.

The doctor was nice; he seemed concerned about her. He knew who she was, since she'd been there many times in the past with Neil. "I think you should sit down. You're still in shock. I'll have the clerk bring you some water."

Water? What good would water do? Why did people always offer water when someone was in shock? All she needed right now was a box of tissues and an empty room, so she could scream and cry her heart out. She had no desire to sit down, either. So as soon as the doctor had turned away from her, she left the hospital and went directly back to her car.

She couldn't drive right away, though. Her vision was too blurry. She could barely see. It was just like that afternoon in the laboratory. Then the tears had been the result of smoke. Now the tears came from an overwhelming grief and sense of loss.

Ever since Neil was born, when he was diagnosed with a rare genetic disorder, she had known this day would eventually come. But knowing didn't make facing the day any easier.

Her whole life had been made up of work and Neil. The work had gone up in smoke that day. And now her beloved Neil was gone too. She had nothing.

So she just sat behind the wheel of her car and cried until there were no more tears left. Great, gasping sobs racked her body.

She had no idea how long she'd spent sitting in her car, but finally she knew she had to pull herself together and go home. She was needed there. Calvin was alone with the baby. Amy, Number Seven, could be hungry, or wet, or just screaming, and Calvin could be in a total panic.

When she returned to her apartment, the baby was

in Calvin's arms, and he wasn't in a panic, but he did seem oddly nervous. And surprised to see her. In fact, he practically jumped at the sight of her when she walked in the door.

"What—what are you doing back here so soon?" he stammered. "Didn't the doctor admit Neil to the hospital? I thought you'd be staying there with him all night, like the last time."

"Neil died, Calvin."

Her neighbor's face crumpled. "No . . . oh, no. Nancy, I'm so sorry!"

"He never regained consciousness," she told him. "He stopped breathing just moments after we arrived at the hospital."

Calvin was clearly shocked and truly shaken by the news. In fact, he was trembling all over. Nancy moved toward him to take the sleeping baby from his arms, and he relinquished her, but he seemed reluctant to do. He edged toward the window and looked out. Nancy thought he was trying to hide his tears.

She tried to console him. "At least he wasn't in any pain, Calvin. He didn't suffer. He died peacefully . . . Calvin, what are you looking at? Is someone out there?" She went to the window and saw a man standing in front of their house. There was something familiar about him. He was looking at the house number, and then, apparently satisfied that he was at the correct address, he started toward the front door.

"Are you expecting someone?" Nancy asked. "Is that a friend of yours?" When Calvin didn't respond, she said, "Oh, I think I know who that must be. It's someone from the hospital. I ran out so fast, without telling anyone that I was leaving, and I was probably supposed to sign some papers."

The door buzzer went off. At the same moment, Amy, Number Seven, opened her eyes and started to cry.

"Calvin, would you go down and get the door? I need to feed the baby." Nancy went into the kitchen and started to prepare a bottle. Moments later she heard footsteps on the staircase and a mumbled conversation coming from the living room. With Amy in one arm and the bottle in her other hand, she went back into the other room.

The visitor was handing Calvin a thick envelope. "You can count it if you want," he said. "It's all there. Fifty thousand dollars."

"What's going on?" Nancy asked.

Calvin looked at her. His expression reminded her of a scared rabbit. She saw fear, and something else. Shame.

Calvin took the envelope and ran out. The man turned to face Nancy, and she gasped in recognition. He wasn't from the hospital. When he had been standing in the darkness outside, she hadn't been able to see the black hair liberally sprinkled with white. It was Ferguson, Mr. Salt-and-Pepper, the Project Crescent accountant who had weekly meetings with Dr. Jaleski at the lab.

"What are you doing here? What do you want?"

"I'm here to retrieve something," the accountant said. "Something you have that belongs to my organization." He stepped toward her. "Give me the clone."

Nancy stepped back. Her head was spinning. "I—I don't understand." She looked over the man's shoulder. Where had Calvin gone?

"Of course you understand," Ferguson said calmly. "You don't own her. *We* paid for the experiment. She's our property. Now, don't make a fuss. Just hand over the clone."

Nancy held the baby tighter. "You're mistaken. This isn't one of the clones, this is my own daughter. The clones were all killed in the explosion. Didn't you hear about that? The laboratory blew up today!"

The man nodded. "Yes, I know all about the explosion. And I also know that you want us to believe the clones were destroyed. And you almost convinced us! But fortunately for us, your baby-sitter was in need of money. He thought we might pay for the information that at least one clone had survived. And he was right." He frowned. "By the way, your baby-sitter is a greedy man. He demanded a lot of money."

Nancy spoke in a whisper. "Enough to buy a Stradivarius?"

"A what? I wouldn't know about that. I have no idea what he's planning to do with the money, and I don't care. But I do know that we paid for a clone. So give her to me, now."

All the time he'd been talking, Nancy had been moving backward. The man didn't appear to have a gun. And back inside the kitchen, there was another door that led out onto a fire escape.

But he could probably run as fast as she could, and the baby in her arms would slow her down. With a sinking heart, Nancy realized that it wouldn't matter whether or not he had a weapon. He was bigger and clearly stronger. He could easily take Amy, Number Seven, from her by force.

And he did. He came forward in a rush and wrenched the baby out of her arms. Nancy screamed, but she knew it wouldn't help. The windows were closed, so who would hear her? The elderly couple upstairs were practically deaf. And downstairs there was only Calvin. He certainly wouldn't be coming to Nancy's aid.

But there was a third person in the room, an unusually strong person. Nancy would never know whether Amy, Number Seven, actually realized what was going on or whether she was simply acting with a normal baby's reflex. In any case, the infant raised a hand—and poked Ferguson right in the eye.

The man let out a howl and staggered back. In the process, he banged his head on the mantel, and this stunned him even more. In that moment of weakness, he started to drop the baby. Nancy rushed forward, grabbed her, and ran out the back door.

Scrambling down the fire escape, she realized that despite all the commotion, the baby wasn't struggling or fussing at all. It was almost as if she was trying to make the escape as easy as possible for Nancy.

Dropping to the ground, Nancy ran around to the front of the house. An obstacle stood there, in the shape of her neighbor and ex-friend. But Nancy was too angry to be frightened. She stared at Calvin in a fury.

"What were you going to tell me when I got back from the hospital and found out that the baby was gone? Were you going to say someone broke in and kidnapped her? Too bad for you that I came back early. I might have believed you."

Calvin said nothing. He didn't even raise his eyes to look at her.

She knew she had to start running. Ferguson would recover from the blow and be outside any minute. And she didn't have the keys to her car. But she couldn't resist one last comment.

"I hope you enjoy your violin, Calvin. You betrayed me for it. I will never forgive you."

And off she ran into the night.

thirteen

"Slow down!" the man was shrieking at Calvin. "You want to kill all of us? Slow down, or the kid here gets it right between the eyes!"

Amy thought he was bluffing. Surely she was worth more to the organization alive than dead. On the other hand, she didn't know that for certain. Maybe a dead clone could be replicated as easily as a live one.

In any case, if the kidnapper didn't kill her, the bus ride just might. They were moving incredibly fast. She thought Calvin might be trying to attract the police by speeding. But apparently there weren't many traffic cops watching for speeding buses in Washington. Or maybe the bus was just too far away from the center of the city. She couldn't tell. Outside was a blur; the scenery flew by too fast for even Amy to make out the location. She thought she caught a glimpse of the Potomac River, though. They seemed to be on a highway just over it.

"Take the next exit!" the man screamed at Calvin.

Calvin did as he was told, but he took the turn so sharply that the man was thrown off balance. He slid along the floor of the bus, skidding almost all the way to the driver's seat.

Amy ran after him. This could be her chance to grab the gun. But if it was, she blew it. Despite her speed, the man was up and back in control before she could make a move for the weapon. "Sit down," he ordered her, indicating the front seat by the door.

She backed away, moving toward the seat. Out of the corner of her eye, she saw that Calvin had his hand on the lever that operated the door. Suddenly she knew what he was about to do.

The bus door swung open. Below her Amy could see the ground rushing past. And now she knew what *she* had to do.

For a split second she wavered. She might be stronger, more flexible, and faster than normal people. But she had never confronted a situation like this. She had no idea whether she could survive the jump.

Apparently Calvin thought she could. "Jump, Amy! Jump!"

She couldn't waste any more time deciding. The man had whirled around, and the gun was pointing directly at her. She jumped.

The sound of a bullet rang in the air, but it didn't reach her. She flew over the railing that hugged the road and hit the ground with a thud that knocked the breath out of her. Then she began to roll downhill.

She rolled over and over, accelerating so fast that she couldn't stop herself. Finally she came to a stop at the bottom of the hill.

She hurt all over, and she didn't know if any bones were broken. Slowly, tentatively, she stretched out an arm and used it as leverage to raise her head. Looking up, she could see the bus as it careened around a curve, then turned again, so sharply that the movement had to have been intentional. It hit the railing and sailed into the air. For a moment it almost seemed as if it was suspended in space. Then it plunged into the Potomac River.

She gazed in wonderment as the bus sank. It was almost as if the river was swallowing it. Then it disappeared, leaving only a few bubbles on the water's surface.

fourteen

Running with a baby in her arms wasn't easy. Nancy didn't have a lot of experience with babies, but she suspected that this one might be heavier than most. On the other hand, Amy, Number Seven, didn't struggle or wail. She remained remarkably still, as if she was purposefully trying to cooperate with the escape effort. Nancy had no idea if Mr. Salt-and-Pepper was behind her, or how close he might be, and she didn't dare take the time to look over her shoulder.

Then, wonder of wonders, a taxi appeared on the quiet street. And it was unoccupied by any passenger.

The second she spotted it, Nancy slowed down to a

walk so the taxi driver wouldn't think she was some kind of crazy person, running through the dark streets with a baby. She flagged him down, and to her immense joy, the taxi came to a stop alongside her.

She jumped into the car and closed the door, and as the taxi began to move, she sank back in the seat and allowed herself a sigh of relief. The relief was only temporary.

"Where to, lady?" the driver asked.

"Excuse me?" she asked.

He spoke slowly and deliberately, as if he thought she was a foreigner who barely spoke English. "Where. Do. You. Want. To. Go?"

It occurred to her that she had no idea where she wanted to go, or where she *could* go. To a hotel, maybe? Then she realized she didn't have her handbag, which meant she didn't have any money or credit cards to pay for a hotel. Or the taxi.

Her silence was making the driver nervous. "Uh, miss? Where am I taking you?"

Thank heavens, she remembered an address. She'd only been there once before, at a staff party, but it was the only place she could think of where she might find a sympathetic ear—and a loan.

Amy, Number Seven, had been so quiet, Nancy assumed she'd fallen asleep. Looking at her now, she saw that the baby's eyes were open and alert. And once again, Nancy could have sworn she saw a glimmer of a smile.

Dr. Jaleski lived in a quiet suburb of the capital, a pretty residential area that seemed like a haven of peace and safety. Nancy was already feeling calmer as the driver pulled up in front of a low ranch-style home.

"Here you are, lady."

"Um, could you wait just a moment?" Nancy asked. "I'll be right back." Without waiting for a response, she slid out of the car and hurried up the walk to the front door.

Please be home, please be home, she begged silently as she knocked. And she hoped he would be home alone. Dr. Jaleski had a wife and a teenage daughter, and Nancy wasn't quite sure how much Dr. Jaleski shared with them about his work.

She was relieved when Dr. Jaleski himself opened the door. "Nancy! What are you doing here?"

She smiled weakly. "I didn't know where else to go."

Behind her, the taxi driver began honking his horn. "Um, I don't have any money," she told Dr. Jaleski.

He didn't ask for an explanation. He ran down the walk, paid the driver, and returned. "Come inside," he said.

The house was quiet, and he appeared to be alone.

135

Ushering her into the kitchen, he looked down at the bundle in her arms. "How is she?"

"Fine, I think. Especially considering what she's experienced today." She told Dr. Jaleski the whole story—about Neil, and Ferguson, and Calvin's betrayal. And as she related the day's events, it hit her—how much *she'd* been through that day. Her voice began to shake.

Dr. Jaleski too was overcome. "Oh, Nancy," he said, his eyes radiating compassion. He took her hand. No other words were necessary, and she knew she had his complete sympathy and concern.

He produced a pillow so Nancy could lay the baby down and give her arms a rest. Then he made some coffee for them, and they sat down at the kitchen table. Dr. Jaleski contemplated the implications of Ferguson's appearance and demand for Amy, Number Seven.

He sighed heavily. "So they know the clones are alive."

"I think they have their suspicions," Nancy told him. "But they only know about this one for sure. I told him this was my own child, but I suppose it would be easy enough for him to check and find out that I don't have any children."

He agreed. Stroking the baby's soft, downy head, he said, "She's not safe here, Nancy. And I don't mean just here, in this house. We have to get her out of the Washington area. As far away as possible."

He was right, and Nancy knew that. But she knew something else, too. Maybe she'd known for a while now, but at that moment, the reality hit her hard. And she spoke it out loud.

"I can't let her go. I want to keep her."

Dr. Jaleski didn't seem shocked or even particularly surprised to hear her say this. But clearly he was disturbed.

"Nancy, do you know what you're getting yourself into? Being a single mother is hard enough as it is. But being the single mother of someone like an Amy— well, that's something else."

"I know."

"No, Nancy, you don't know, you can't possibly know." He gazed at her with an intensity she'd never before seen on his face. "Listen to me, and listen carefully. Amy, Number Seven, is an experiment."

"She's still a human being—" Nancy began to say, but he interrupted her.

"Yes, she's a human being, but she's a kind of human being that hasn't existed before now. We have no idea what the future holds for her. We don't know what she'll be like tomorrow, or the next day, or the next year."

"You could say the same thing about any baby," Nancy pointed out. "They are all different. You never know how they're going to behave, what they'll grow up to be."

"That's true," he admitted. "But you can make some assumptions. If children are generally healthy, there are some fairly accurate predictions that can be made about their physical and mental development. We know approximately when that child will be able to walk, when that child will begin speaking. We can estimate the age at which certain thought processes will develop. With these clones—we don't even know if they will age normally!"

Nancy gazed down at the infant, who was now sleeping peacefully. "She looks like any normal baby."

"But we don't know how her special genetic structure will cause her to develop," Dr. Jaleski said. "The altered genes may produce accelerated growth hormones. Two years from now, you could find yourself the mother of a ten-year-old!"

"Or the mother of a two-year-old," Nancy countered. "Like you said, we can't make any predictions. Maybe she'll be perfect."

Dr. Jaleski rubbed his forehead, as if all this contemplation was giving him a massive headache. "There are so many possibilities. Her body may not be able to cope with the demands of her complex cellular makeup. Her heart may not be capable of supporting her growth.

You just lost your brother, Nancy. Are you prepared to deal with the premature death of yet another beloved child?"

Nancy answered that question promptly and honestly. "No. No one can be prepared for something like that. And if she doesn't survive very long, that will be tragic, and I'll be devastated. Just as I was devastated earlier this evening. And I might not be able to recover from another tragedy like that." She paused to take a deep breath and met Dr. Jaleski's eyes squarely. "But I'm willing to take that risk."

Dr. Jaleski wasn't going to give up the argument. He seemed determined to talk her out of this. "I want you to ask yourself a question, Nancy. Why do you want to do this? Why do you want to take on this responsibility? To replace Neil?"

"No," Nancy said. "Neil can't be replaced, ever."

"Because you want to be a mother?" he suggested.

She considered this. "Because I want to be the mother of this child," she finally replied. "From the very beginning, when all the Amys were in their incubators, I felt a strange, special bond with this one. Don't ask me how or why. I can't be logical about it. It's a feeling. Like when you fall in love. You can't explain it, you just *feel* it."

Dr. Jaleski couldn't argue with that. But he wasn't

finished. "One more thing, Nancy. There could be a great deal of danger involved in raising this child. Danger for her and for you, too. If the organization that funded the project believes that even one clone survived that explosion, they will be looking for her. If they are sincerely committed to creating a master race and taking over the world, they won't give up the search. To protect her, you're going to have to keep her identity a secret. From *everybody*. Maybe even from the child herself."

"But how could that be possible?" Nancy asked. "If she isn't like other kids, she'll *know* there's something different about her."

"Then you're going to have to think of a way to explain her differences to her, and to anyone else who notices. But her identity must remain a secret. If you are threatened by the organization, you'll have to deal with it yourself. You can't go to the police, you can't get a lawyer, because you can't tell anyone about her. Remember, you'll not only be protecting her, you will be protecting the world from that organization. No one can ever know that we have created genetically designed clones."

"No one will ever know," Nancy promised him, with more assurance than she really felt.

"All right." Dr. Jaleski rose from the table. "We've got

work to do. First of all, you have to get out of town tonight. Now. Where will you go?"

"I'm not sure," Nancy said.

"You went to a university in California for your undergraduate degree, didn't you?" Dr. Jaleski asked. "You can go back out there. It's a big state with some big cities. You'll be able to find a job." He picked up the phone and dialed a number. "Hello, I'd like to make a reservation on your next flight to Los Angeles. One way." Once the flight had been arranged, he told Nancy he would lend her money to get started out in Los Angeles. "I'll make up a birth certificate for the child," he said. "And I'll call a cab to take you to the airport. But after that . . . you're going to be pretty much on your own, Nancy. Think you can handle it?"

Nancy rose and picked up Amy, Number Seven. The baby was awake now, and she was looking straight at Nancy. "We're on our own, Amy. What do you think of that?"

She didn't think the child was so advanced that she would actually respond. But this time, she was absolutely, positively sure that Amy, Number Seven, was smiling.

fifteen

The light breeze that blew through the cemetery wasn't cold, but Amy shivered anyway. "And you left Washington that same night."

"Yes," her mother said. "It was a long flight, and I spent the time making up a story to tell people. And to tell you, when you were old enough to ask."

Amy knew the story about a husband in the military, a husband who had died before his daughter was born, and a fire that had destroyed all mementos of that marriage. She'd believed it all, too, until just about a year before, when she'd begun to notice how different she was, how much stronger she was than her friends.

How she could learn faster, see farther, do so many things better than anyone else her age could. Her recurring nightmare, the one in which she was trapped in a glass cage, surrounded by fire, prompted her to ask questions. A school assignment to have students write their autobiography prompted even more. And the more questions she asked, the more discoveries she made. Finally Nancy had to tell her the truth. Most of it, at least. Now Amy thought she knew it all.

"So that was how Calvin betrayed you. He alerted the organization that you had saved me from the explosion."

"Yes. I didn't think I would ever forgive him." Nancy gazed at the new grave in front of them and the small, plain marker that identified its occupant. "But I forgive him now. He made up for his betrayal."

There hadn't been many people at Calvin's funeral—just some relatives and a few coworkers. And Nancy and Amy. The minister who conducted the service and said the prayers had never known Calvin personally. No mention was made of how Calvin had died.

Amy looked at her mother. "You think he drove that bus into the Potomac River on purpose, don't you?"

Nancy nodded. "He knew enough about how you were created to think you had a good chance of surviving a jump from the bus. And he knew that the hijacker, whoever he was, would just come back after you. So he did the only thing he could think of to save you."

Amy could only gaze in awe at the grave of the man who had sacrificed his life for her. She whispered, "Thank you," but it didn't seem like enough. How could a person ever express gratitude for such a gift?

Nancy opened her handbag and took out a folded paper. Amy recognized it as the note Calvin had given her. "I think I'm ready to read this now," her mother said. She unfolded the paper.

Amy watched her mother's face as she read. She was pleased when her mother began to share some of the note with her.

" 'I've lived in torment, knowing what I did to you,' " she read out loud. " 'With the money I received from that man, I bought a Stradivarius, but I don't think I had one moment of pleasure with it. I went into a deep depression, utter despair, and I began using drugs to wipe out my memories. As I became addicted to drugs, I lost my job, and I stopped making music. Eventually I had to sell the violin for my drug habit. I'm not telling you this because I want your sympathy. I would never ask you to forgive me. I can never forgive myself.' "

Amy didn't think she'd ever heard anything so sad in

her life. True, Calvin had done an awful thing, but he'd paid dearly for his mistake.

Nancy went on reading in silence. Then she drew in her breath sharply. "Ohmigod."

"What does it say?" Amy wanted to know.

Her mother looked sick. "I always wondered how Calvin knew *who* to call that night. I'd never told him the names of anyone in the organization. He didn't even know the name of the project. But he'd met Grace, over dinner, at my apartment."

Amy gasped. "He called Grace Morrison to find out who he could sell me to?"

Nancy's voice hardened. "No. Grace called him. She saw me leave the laboratory with you. She couldn't bear to stop working on the clones, and she would have cooperated with that evil organization rather than completely abandon the project."

"So Dr. Hopkins was right about her," Amy said.

Nancy nodded. "I'm thinking now that she would have sold her soul to the devil for a chance to make science history." Her face was grim as she refolded the paper. "She knew we were going to go the FBI building. She must have figured out the route the buses would take. So she knew exactly where the man should wait to hijack the bus."

"How evil!" Amy burst out. "What are we going to do about her, Mom?"

"There's nothing we can do, sweetie. It's like Dr. Jaleski warned me almost thirteen years ago. I can't go to the police and report her."

Amy sighed. Her mother was right, of course, but it was so frustrating to be powerless. "Let's go home, Mom. Let's go back to L.A. Today." The rest of the seventh grade had already left. Only she and her mother had stayed for Calvin's funeral.

"We'll leave today," her mother told her. "But there's something I want to show you here first."

For once Amy didn't object when her mother took her hand. Amy had a feeling she knew where they were going and that her mother would need some support when they got there.

Together they went to the stone that marked the grave of Neil Candler and stood there silently.

"Uncle Neil," Amy said. "I wish I could have known him."

Nancy spoke softly. "Dr. Jaleski took care of everything after I left. This is the first time I've seen where Neil . . ." Her voice trailed off.

Amy tightened her grip on her mother's hand. "He was the only family you had."

"Yes." Nancy wiped away a tear.

Amy felt like crying too. "Oh, Mom, it must have been horrible for you. How did you deal with it? Some people would just fall apart if something like that happened."

"I couldn't fall apart, Amy. I had become a mother, and I had a daughter to look after."

"Thanks for taking care of me, Mom."

"You're welcome, Amy. I hope I've been doing a good job."

"Oh, you have," Amy assured her. "And you won't have to work so hard at taking care of me in the future."

"Why do you say that?"

"I'm almost thirteen, Mom. I'm about to become a real teenager."

Her mother didn't seem to be too thrilled at the prospect. "You know, Amy, adolescence can be a rough time. And something tells me that a genetically engineered teen won't be any easier to handle than an ordinary one."

"Don't be silly," Amy scoffed. "I'm so much more mature and advanced than other kids my age. I can take care of myself. You'll be able to give me a lot more freedom. And I won't need any supervision at all. Of course, it would help if I got a substantial increase in my allowance. Mom, why are you looking at me like that?"

"Oh, Amy," Nancy moaned. "Are you going to be a typical teen?"

Amy grinned. "Hey, Mom, I was never a typical child. What makes you think I'm going to be any more typical as a teen?"

Don't miss

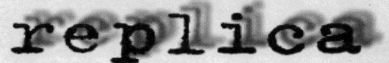

#15
Transformation

Something's wrong with Tasha—she's not herself. At least that's what Amy thinks. And a best friend would know! Tasha's eyes look glazed. Her usual quick comebacks have become dull one-word answers. It's as if Tasha is acting out some part in a horror movie. Only this isn't a movie, it's real.

One by one, Amy notices other personality changes. The people Amy loves just aren't themselves. Everyone seems possessed!

And soon . . . whatever's happening to them may happen to Amy too.